CHARLY'S
EPICFIASCOS

Star
Power

Also by Kelli London

Charly's Epic Fiascos Series

Charly's Epic Fiascos

Reality Check

Boyfriend Season Series

Boyfriend Season

Cali Boys

Uptown Dreams

The Break-Up Diaries, Vol. 1 (with Ni-Ni Simone)

Published by Kensington Publishing Corporation

CHARLY'S
EPICFIASCOS
Star
Power

KELLI LONDON

Dafina KTeen Books
KENSINGTON PUBLISHING CORP.
http://www.kensingtonbooks.com

DAFINA KTEEN BOOKS are published by

Kensington Publishing Corp.
119 West 40th Street
New York, NY 10018

All Kensington titles, imprints, and distributed lines are available at special quantity discounts for bulk purchases for sales promotion, premiums, fund-raising, educational, or institutional use.

Special book excerpts or customized printings can also be created to fit specific needs. For details, write or phone the office of the Kensington Special Sales Manager: Attn.: Special Sales Department. Kensington Publishing Corp., 119 West 40th Street, New York, NY 10018. Phone: 1-800-221-2647.

KTeen logo Reg. US Pat. & TM Off.
Sunburst logo Reg. US Pat. & TM Off.

ISBN-13: 978-0-7582-8699-4
ISBN-10: 0-7582-8699-6
First Printing: August 2013

eISBN-13: 978-0-7582-8700-7
eISBN-10: 0-7582-8700-3
First Electronic Edition: August 2013

10 9 8 7 6 5 4 3 2 1

Printed in the United States of America

T
C2
K,
You
three
are:
360˚
MC2
IS
RA
EL
!

Acknowledgments

To my fantastic trio, the epitome of everything wonderful and good.

To the world's most loving mom (my mom)!

My family and friends: you know who you are and how much you mean.

Selena James: your creative mind is truly appreciated!

To the real spirit behind Dr. Deveraux: El, you are a true navigator of the Morning Star!

For my readers: As always, I truly and humbly thank you with all of my heart. You're incredible and appreciated.

And for you, [*insert your name here*]: I thank you for all your support, for reading *all* of my books, and for being the dedicated reader you are. You are truly the best and so amazing.

Take care. Be strong. Love yourself.

Your girl,

Kells
Kellilondon.com

A note from Kelli

Writing the Charly's Epic Fiascos series has been rewarding and enlightening. Through Charly's life and adventures, I've been faced with making many decisions for Charly that I wouldn't have necessarily made for myself. However, as with real life, swaying toward right or wrong—what others deem as correct or incorrect—isn't always necessary. As a wonderful sister-friend pointed out to me, it's not always about right or wrong—it's about what's best. Oftentimes, that's what we have to do (what's best), even if it doesn't fit neatly into society's classification box of appropriate versus inappropriate. After all, who said we only have two options from which to choose? Maybe, just maybe, our decisions lie between the two—choices which someone or something came up with, which means, to me, that we have the option of choosing from their options or not.

Now, I'm not encouraging anyone to break rules. I'm pushing for making the best decisions based upon what you have, your research, what you know to be true, and what feels right because the answers lie within. I'm a firm believer in listening to your instinct, not to the majority. *Majority* is just another word for popular and, as you're about to discover, popular isn't always the way to go.

So the point of this note is for you to do what's best for

you—not what others are or aren't doing. Don't try to fit into the world; make the world fit you. You are the best person you know and, if not, make yourself the best person you know, then share that goodness with everyone else.

I believe in you!

Chat soon,
Kells

1

Asinine, that's what they all were. With an emphasis on
the first syllable, Charly thought, stuffing a mustard-
colored envelope into her oversized hippie bag while jogging down the stairwell. Anger moved her, pushing her
faster, literally and emotionally. Adrenaline fed her strength
as she pulled open the door and made it bounce off the
wall as if it weren't made of heavy metal. She stumbled
into the building lobby without the least bit of embar-
rassment. She was too upset to care if anyone saw her almost bust her butt; the only thing that mattered was
them not catching up to her. Them being her dad and Mr.
Day and all their other suited and booted flunkies who'd
converged to decide what should happen with *her* life
and career. They'd all seemed to agree with her father's
demand that she *had* to—not should—stay on the honor
roll to continue acting, then she was handed the envelope
with the agreement they'd signed, edging her to look it

over right before she'd excused herself to go to the rest room. But she wasn't going to the bathroom; she was breaking camp—getting out of there as soon as possible to avoid *their* demands and contract. *It's my life, not theirs,* and *It's not even acting* moved through her mind as her eyes looked left, then right, scanning faces. She didn't want to see anyone she knew, and she didn't. "Thank God," surged out from her lungs, sounding more like a whoosh than a word, making her realize she had been holding her breath during her escape.

"Ms. St. James," the building concierge greeted from behind the semicircle reception desk.

"Hello," Charly said, speeding past, then halting, her long black tresses swishing from the sudden stop. She backtracked. She needed him. "Can you do me a favor, please?" she asked, making her way to the desk, and lightly tapping her manicured nails on the surface. She blinked her long lashes slowly and smiled, making her baby browns twinkle. "It's my boss's birthday, and I'm the lucky one who gets to go pick up his gift." She flipped over her wrist and looked at her watch. She stretched her eyes until they saucered, then exhaled as if frustrated about the time. "He'll probably send one of his assistants, who aren't in on the surprise, to come looking for me. They think we have a meeting soon. It's a diversion though . . ." She bit her lip, trying to finish the lie. "Me and the cast couldn't think of any other way to get him out of the office while they set up one of the conference rooms for the surprise." She widened her grin, pleased with her gift for performing.

The concierge nodded and grinned. "That's nice, Ms.

St. James. Don't worry. I got'cha. I'm usually the gift runner too. If anyone comes looking for you, I haven't seen a thing," he said, playfully covering his eyes.

Charly dug in her hippie bag, then slid him a twenty. "Thanks. I appreciate it," she said, then turned and hurried through the lobby.

Hot wind met her face as soon as she exited, pushing her hair back. Tears started to form in her eyes as her anger rose to the surface, but they dried as quickly as they came. The temperature had to be almost a hundred. How dare they do that to her? she questioned, quickening her pace, keeping up with other always-in-a-rush New Yorkers. She'd been doing her best, studying whenever she could, and had rarely been seen without a textbook. Grades had been at the forefront of it all, and she hadn't slacked. Well, not totally. She only took a much-needed break to shop, Skype, text, and work on keeping her facial expressions in check. That's what the studio had requested; that she tame her emotions—the negative ones—while she was on camera. Other than that, she'd been all work and no play, and was glad June had finally rolled in and rolled out the red carpet for her summertime freedom. Now she could focus on what she loved best without interruption from online classes—getting ready for the new season of *The Extreme Dream Team*.

People brushed against her without apology, making her realize she'd slowed her pace and was in the way. She refocused, deciding not to let her dad and the others' decisions about her life get to her. They could say what they wanted, but at the end of the day, she'd get her way. Period. She just needed to figure out how. And fitting that puzzle

together required her form of therapy—shoe shopping.
Yep, a new pair would be just what she needed to remix
her day into something good, she decided, making her
way to the curb and raising her arm out to hail a cab.

"Hi, Charly!" someone greeted, snatching her attention.

Charly paused and looked over her shoulder. She exhaled and smiled. "Hi, how are you?" she sang to a dowdy
teenager. The girl's face looked around seventeen years
old, but the rest of her looked ancient. Her hair was in
need of a style and her clothes were a hodgepodge of dis-
asters. The colors matched, but that was it. "It's nice to
see you," Charly said, wishing she could take the girl
home and make her over. She'd never seen her before, but
she'd greeted her like she had. Being a television personality, she had gotten used to doing what she'd been
taught not to do—talk to strangers. But in her line of
work, she learned there was no such thing as a stranger.
The viewers were more like friends who felt they knew
her, so she made it a point to make them feel like they
did.

"I'm great now!" the girl answered gleefully, sticking
her hand in a terribly outdated purse that lacked anything remotely close to being called cute. "Can I please
have your—"

"Sure, it'll be my pleasure," Charly said, answering the
question before the girl completed it.

The girl whipped out a piece of paper, but had a blank
look on her face, which only highlighted her bushy eyebrows. "I just had it. I must've left my pen . . ."

If I had those eyebrows, they'd be arched to the max.

And that skin . . . her eyes . . . Does she not know how much of a gem she could be with some polishing? Charly thought. She nodded, then fished in her hippie bag. She shook her head. "I don't have one either," she explained. She really wanted to be in a cab by now, but the shoes would have to wait. Viewers came first, and she was thankful that anyone wanted her autograph at all. To her she was just Charly from the Midwest, not the big star fans treated her as. "Sorry." Her apology was genuine. She felt bad she couldn't sign her autograph for the girl, and even sorrier that she couldn't help her pretty up.

The girl locked eyes with her, and the look behind them was a mix of happiness and sadness. "I was just in there." She pointed to a nearby frozen yogurt shop. Charly noticed her uneven nails. "And I must've left it with Liam. I just got his autograph. It'd be great if I could have both of yours."

Charly smiled. She could use a dose of Liam now. Liam and frozen yogurt and shoes. Charly walked away from the curb. "Okay. You got it. Let's go!"

"Oh my God. Really?" the girl asked, staying in step with Charly. "I had no idea you'd be so cool. I did, but you know," she began and didn't stop until Charly's hand was pulling open the door to the yogurt shop.

"Charly. Charly. Charly!" Liam sang, walking toward the door and taking Charly's breath away. His tall, athletic and muscular build was luring. His cocoa brown complexion had bronzed with his tan, making his amber brown eyes seem lighter, and perfect white teeth gleem. He had a huge container of yogurt in his hand and a

smile on his face. "Oh, and you. How are you? You forgot this," he said, whipping out a pen from his back
pocket.

Charly took the pen from him, reached for the paper
from the girl, then signed it. "It was so nice to meet you.
Thank you for watching the show."

The girl wrapped her arms around Charly and squeezed,
then she did the same to Liam, but held on longer. "Oh.
Sorry," she said, letting him go and apologizing to
Charly. "I forgot this is your man. But you can't blame
me. He's gorgeous . . . but so are you. You make a good
couple," she stammered, backtracking to the door.

Charly grinned, silently agreeing with the girl on Liam
being gorgeous, then waved good-bye. "Thank you. And
you're pretty too. You are," she said, really meaning it.
The girl was pretty underneath all her layers of drab and
outdated fashion, terrible hair and bushy brows. "Don't
forget to watch the show!" she said as the girl left. She
turned to Liam and laced her arm through his. "I need
you. I need you and something cold and incredible shoes.
ASAP."

"Uh-oh," he said, unlacing his arm from hers, then
giving her a tight hug. "Tell it all to big daddy," he
teased. He pulled back, then looked at her. "Why'd you
lie to the little girl?" he asked. "You can't just go around
giving compliments just because someone wants your autograph."

Charly laughed, then loosened his grip and waved away
his comment. "She is pretty. She just doesn't know or
show it. And she's not a little girl. She has to be at least

seventeen." She walked to the counter and grabbed a container for her frozen yogurt.

"Try fourteen," he said, following behind her as she made her way to the wall where she filled her container with vanilla.

"Get out," Charly said, going to the toppings station. "She's not. Where'd you get that?"

"She told me."

Charly poured scoops of almonds on top of granola and strawberries, then walked to the cashier to get her frozen treat weighed. "Serious?"

"Don't you dare reach for your wallet. Gentlemen don't let ladies pay." He reached into his pocket, then paid the cashier. He looked at Charly and nodded. "Serious, love. Fourteen."

"Liam, that's awful. I could make her a whole new girl. I'm talking fantabulous. From her head to her heels." She scooped a spoonful into her mouth.

"You know you're on the wrong show, don't ya, love? You need to be hosting a makeover show. Charly got a mean walk, a mean shoe game." He sang a Fat Joe and Chris Brown song, replacing his own lyrics for theirs, but keeping the melody. He laughed. "I've been in the States too long."

Charly blushed. "Thanks. It would be kinda hot to host a makeover show, but I don't have time for that. At least not now," she said, thinking she wouldn't be hosting any show—*The Extreme Dream Team* or any other— if she didn't pull up her grades to the adults' satisfaction. "So what about going to get the shoes?" she asked, trying to keep the light mood going. She didn't want to give herself another second to think about her dad and the envelope, so she stayed focused on new kicks.

Liam crinkled his brows. "Wait! I forgot to tell you that they tried to pigeonhole me for the new tapings. They said I have to *get* on the honor roll to keep my career." He laughed. "I had to remind them that I turned down a scholarship—an Ivy League one at that—that I was offered because of rowing *and* academics. Seems they're trying to make it some new policy . . . We can thank your dad for that, love. Huh? Good thing I've never gotten below a B."

Get? Get? Get? churned over and over through Charly's mind. "Did you say you have to *get* on the honor roll or *stay* on it?" she asked, just to be clear.

Liam shook his head. "Technically, they should've said *stay,* but they said I have to *get* on it."

"Here," she said, handing him her frozen yogurt. She grabbed his arm, pulled him out of the way of someone walking through the door, then reached into her bag. She took out the oversized envelope. *You have to stay on the honor roll to continue acting.* That's what she remembered them saying before they handed her the agreement. *Right?* she questioned her memory. "You have to get, I have to *stay,*" she said, then unfolded the envelope. She looked at Liam, who wore a puzzled expression. "I think I have to work on not overreacting. It interferes with my hearing." She opened the flap, then pulled out the contract. On top of it was a copy of her report card that she hadn't seen and didn't realize had been sent out. A smile parted her lips. She nodded. "I'm good, Liam. Three Bs, and those are my lowest scores. I'm on the honor roll! C'mon. We have to get back to Mr. Day's office."

"I thought we were going to buy you some shoes. You know, get you prepared to work on your fashion dos and don'ts for the next series you'll be hosting," he joked.

Charly took her yogurt and laughed, but her glee wasn't in a joking manner. Liam had sparked an idea. If the Suits and Boots—her name for the adults who felt they made the rules—had demands, couldn't she also? "Who needs shoes when we've got a new series coming up? A series I think we should have some say about. Let's go. I'll fill you in on the way."

"There," Charly said, sliding a piece of paper across Mr. Day's desk. It bore both her and Liam's signatures. "That's the contract we're proposing." Charly sat back, crossing her legs. She looked over at Liam, who nodded in agreement.

"It's a hot idea, Day." Liam backed Charly.

Mr. Day picked up the piece of paper, then pressed his lips together in thought as he looked at it. He rotated in his chair, then reached forward, and dialed numbers on his phone. "Can you come in here? Now?" he said into his headset. He disconnected, then looked at Charly. He sat and didn't say a word. His silence made the room uncomfortable.

Charly looked at Liam, who only shrugged and pierced her eyes with his. There was a slight knock on the door, then one of the Suits and Boots walked in.

"What's up?" the man said to Mr. Day.

Mr. Day handed him the piece of paper, and the man

looked it over. "Who's responsible for this?" His eyes met Charly's, then Liam's.

Charly and Liam looked at one another, then turned to him. Both said, "We are."

Mr. Day exhaled, then looked to the other man. "Okay. Pitch it, Charly."

Charly pointed to her chest. "Me? But we both . . ." She looked at Liam, and he nodded his approval. His eyes silently told her she could do it, he had faith in her.

"A'ight," she exclaimed, with sass and strength. "I got this, babe," she said to Liam. "*The Extreme Dream Team* special summer edition show. We'll take the life of a loner, make them go from drab to fab, and turn them into a VIP. I'm talking complete makeover—attitude, self-confidence and self-esteem, clothes, and . . ." She looked at Liam. "New digs, of course. I'll rework the person, Liam and the rest of the crew will rework their space. We'll make the person feel good, look good, and live good. You know, finally work on the gift *inside* the package. We always wrap a pretty package—someone's space, but what about the person? Who wants to live good and not look and feel good?"

"It's not technically true, but I'd say it's close to an oxymoron," Liam said.

"Well, Charly—" Mr. Day began.

"Mr. Day," she interrupted, cutting him off. She stood and placed both of her hands on his desk, then leaned forward. "Our ratings are high—at least they were for the last shows—the one that me and Liam hosted, and the reruns too. We don't want to lose that. Do we?"

"Well—" Mr. Day began.

"No, we don't," Charly said, cutting him off again. "Besides, we gave you what you wanted and what my dad demanded. We got a hot show on our hands and, as you know, I didn't come here—"

Mr. Day slammed his hand down on his desk, the pound making the room grow quiet. "Charly! Please? You didn't come here for *nothing*. You've been telling me that forever now. I know!" He laughed, and the staff relaxed under his grin. "If you didn't have so much spunk—and that mouth—you would've let me finish." He looked at Liam, then back to Charly. He winked. The other man clapped. "You and you"—he said, pointing to Charly, then Liam—"have just solved our dilemma. We wanted a new twist—that's what we were meeting about when you disappeared and went to the bathroom—and you delivered it."

"So how do you propose we do it?" the other man asked.

Liam sat up. He shrugged. "Easy, mate. You're the network, so network it. Run a couple of ads—radio and on the telly, and have someone nominated."

2

TALLULAHVILLE
POPULATION 1,257

Charly settled against the backseat of the town car, and prepared for the second leg of her trip. They were going to Tallulahville, a town just outside of Minneapolis, Minnesota, which was sixty-plus miles from civilization and the airport. The flight from New York had been uneventful, but, as usual, she couldn't sleep on the plane, and was now anxious and tired. She was excited about the upcoming show, and couldn't wait to begin the drab-to-fab makeover, but sleep was calling her. She yawned and stretched. She needed rest now more than ever. Nia, the winner of the contest, who had no idea she was getting a total overhaul or that she had even been entered into a contest, had been called difficult and resistant. From the pictures Charly had seen, she knew

Nia was going to be a heavy project, but she was up for the challenge, which would begin as soon as her feet touched the pavement. Charly looked at her watch, calculating time and distance. If she guessed correctly, that meant she had at least an hour to nap, if she were lucky. She didn't have long to work her magic, but she wouldn't complain. She'd get the task done, and was thankful the opportunity had come. It'd taken almost a month for the studio to select a winner, but finally the time had come for Charly to show the world her other gift: the ability to make over someone from the inside. She opened the folder sitting on her lap, and looked at Nia's photos that had been submitted with her other information. Her hair was pulled back in a braid, and from what Charly could see, it was a yucky dull-brown that bordered on dirty looking. Her eyes were large, outlined with barely there lashes, and her heart-shaped face held not an ounce of love, but was weighed down by brows that looked inherited from Bert from *Sesame Street,* and a jagged scar was on her cheek. In one phrase, Charly summed her up: She looked as if she'd been dipped in frown juice. Charly shook her head, realizing how big a task she'd be undertaking soon. But she could do it. Somewhere under the weary mask of depression the girl Nia wore, Charly was sure there lived a pretty girl. Nia was plain and drab, but workable. Charly was certain she could snatch Nia out of the hole she'd climbed into after surviving a terrible car accident that'd left her face and confidence scarred as her story suggested. She was also a nerd, having never received anything less than an A+.

"You ready, love? I know it's going to be a difficult

time for you because Marlow couldn't come. It's too bad they're allergic to dogs," Liam said, climbing into the car and sitting beside her. She and Liam and two cameramen, who were in a different town car, had flown in a day earlier than the rest of the cast so they could scout locations and goods and check out the businesses who'd offered their services. And the cameramen had another task; they were to act as guardians. That's what Mr. Day had said. But Charly didn't care, and she wasn't too focused on the scouting; she was concerned with the hair salon and spa and, above all else, the department stores. Liam needed to meet with locals who'd help him and Sully, his co-host construction sidekick, fix Nia's structure—a room they'd turn into a full-fledged library and technology room—while Charly met with Nia's family and friends, namely Rory, the one who'd nominated her, to find out who Nia really was. She was sure that beneath all of Nia's nesses—introvertedness, nerdiness, and drabness—there had to be a gem she could polish until it shone. If there wasn't, that meant Charly would fail. Epically.

Charly looked at him and nodded. She closed the folder. "I know. I'm going to miss my baby, Marlow. My sister and the rest of the crew too, but I'm going to stay as focused as I can on this show. That should help. And to answer your question, I'm as ready as I'll ever be. I just hope the fake mission this town thinks we're on really works. Do you think we can pull it off? I mean if the people in this town think we're here to make over the mayor's office . . ." she began, forgetting the lie the studio had come up with so she could get close to Nia, and make the makeover seem like an accident. She wasn't happy about having to perform a sneak-makeover, but had been told it was the only way. The girl seemed to be resistant to standing out front. "I guess I just don't understand why we'd be renovating the *mayor's* office to get to this girl. I mean, I know she's the mayor's daughter, but overhauling a publicly funded space makes no sense. I'd be upset if my tax money went to rehabbing someone's home."

Liam nodded. "The mayor's private office that me and Sully are turning into space for Nia, remember? The community will know the truth soon, and they won't be mad." He filled her in on what she'd forgotten. "Remember, the mayor's real office caught fire so, temporarily, he's been working from home. It seems he's a tightwad with his budget and doesn't want to waste the community's money, so that makes sense. He has to have somewhere to be mayor from, right?"

Charly shrugged, then laughed. She was more tired than she thought. Now she remembered. Nia's dad did have another office, which was currently being renovated, and he was working from home so he wouldn't have to use tax dollars on a temporary office until the rehab was finished. It just hadn't been announced yet. "Okay, that works. I get it now. You and Sully will be in there making over her dad's personal office for Nia, and I'll be waving my magic wand over Nia."

"Yep. Now you got it." Liam reached over and took the folder from Charly. He opened it and frowned at Nia's picture. "I hope your wand is powerful, love. I really do, because what I'm looking at is not attractive. At all. She reminds me a lot of the girl we met at the frozen yogurt shop, but that girl had an excuse—she was a lot younger and, I bet, her dad isn't the mayor of New York or anywhere else." He shut the folder, then shuddered.

Charly snatched back the folder. "Thanks a lot, Liam. And Nia's not that bad, I betcha. Though I must agree she does kinda resemble the yogurt-shop girl. But I can do this, Liam. I just need a power nap, and I'm good."

"You need a power nap, all right. A power nap and my tools. If this Nia character looks anything in person like she does in the photographs, the girl needs a wall built around her so no one will be able to see her. That's the only way you're gonna help her—you must hide her."

Charly rolled her eyes. "See, that's why you're single. The wrapping is good, but the package is empty." She faked a sneer. "Nia's going to be good. Trust me. She's gonna fake it 'til she makes it. That's my plan. I'm going to get her to act the part until she truly becomes the player. You just watch, I'm going to make her shine."

Liam laughed. "The package isn't empty, love. But we don't have to discuss that. You know you want me." He winked. Charly waved him away. "So your assistant isn't going to help you make her shine?" he asked.

Charly's irises spun fire. As far as she knew, the personal makeover part of the show was hers. She and only she alone would make over Nia; everyone else was either there to assist her or there to help Liam and Sully with the room renovation. "Who? What assistant?" she asked, her attitude beginning to inflate. She'd only been told that making over Nia was her assignment, and she had it in writing. "I didn't agree to an assistant, Liam.

That's not in my contract!" She shook her head. "I hope these people don't make me go to court."

"Court?" Liam questioned, his eyes wide with curiosity. "Surely, you wouldn't." He laughed loudly. "You'd actually take them to court over an assistant?"

Charly nodded, her nostrils flaring. "Yep, but not a court of law—I hold court in the street where the winner takes all. No judge. No jury. Just me and them and these." She held up her fists in the air. "And they better be careful, 'cause I'm nice with these and ain't lost a case yet. That goes for you too, Liam, if you keep laughing. I didn't agree to an assistant. Period."

Liam's smile grew wider. "Sure you did, love."

Charly's neck rotated as her head swerved back and forth like it was going to spin off. "No, I did not," she began.

Liam laughed again. "Calm down, love. Yes, you did. You did when you agreed to us coming here before everyone else. I'm your assistant." He winked. "Don't you want me to assist, I mean, accompany you today? I'll make it worth your while," he flirted.

Charly rolled her eyes, relaxing. "I thought you were just coming to scout for your part."

Liam shook his head. "Nope. I've been assigned to be the diversion—ya know, in case you get mobbed. It seems as if everyone wants to be a part of the show. Tomorrow I'll begin working my end."

Charly smiled. She could live with having Liam around. They weren't together and hadn't shared anything more than the special moment or two followed by the kiss, but she remembered it. How could she forget? she questioned as her eyes moved to his grin. She blinked slowly while reminiscing. His lips had been soft then, and she was sure they still were now, but she wouldn't say anything. There hadn't been closure, and he hadn't pushed the issue, so neither would she. "Okay, assistant. Wake me up when we get there." She winked, shut her eyes, then warmed when she heard his response.

"Anything for you, love. Anything at all. Just say it."

She felt her body rise, then fall. A weird rubbing sound followed. Charly sat up, then stretched. Apparently the town car had rubbed against the curb when parking. She lifted her glasses, then squinted her eyes. Surely, her sight was betraying her. Yes, she'd agreed it would be a good idea to travel to a small town, but she hadn't meant so tiny that she could blink and miss it. Small shops, a gas station/convenience store, and a renovated office building that served as a post office and police precinct sat on the opposite side of the street. Charly gasped, almost afraid to turn her head. She lowered her shades, then cupped her hand on the side of them. She didn't want to see where they were staying. If it was as small-town as everything else before her, she knew she wouldn't want to stay there.

Liam's foot bumped against hers. "You okay, love? The sun bothering you?"

Charly's head rotated in the negative. She pointed toward the side of the street where they were parked. "How does it look? The motel?"

Liam pressed his lips together, then let out a long

"Hmm." Charly's eyes bulged, and Liam laughed. "Nah, it's not that bad. And it's not a motel, it's a hotel. A quaint one, actually. No outside hallways, I promise," he said in a teasing tone.

Charly gave him a sinister smile, then scrunched her nose at him. "You better be right, Liam. You know I'm not a fan of outside corridors and entryways," she said, then reached for the door handle, never taking her eyes off him. He'd taken up most of her power nap, intruding in a dream where he'd tried to kiss her and told her he wanted her to be his girlfriend.

"Wait!" he said loudly, stopping her from opening the door all the way. "Turn around before you get out. There's a mob of people on the corner. I guess they thought we were staying at a hotel down there." He reached over her, grabbed the passenger door, and pulled it shut. He looked over his shoulder and his expression twisted into a look Charly didn't recognize. "From here, they look weird. It's like they have on costumes or something. I can't tell from where we're sitting. Let me get out first. I'd rather them swamp me than you, especially with the way they look." He flexed his muscles. "Besides, I can keep them off."

Charly turned and looked out the back window. Sure enough, there was a weird-looking group gathered. Some were colored blue and silver, others were holding signs that she couldn't make out, but could tell that they were clearly there for them because one sign read CHARLY. She shook her head. "News travels fast. Thanks," she said, turning back to Liam. Her eyes did a quick inspection of his toned body. Yes, he could keep them off. She didn't know how he'd kept himself busy when they were apart, but it definitely included pumping iron. His muscles had obvious clear cuts like sliced bread; his upper body was chiseled and defined. She almost touched him to see how tight his arms were, but she stopped herself. His taut body had been built last year, and as good as he looked, she knew he couldn't do anything but improve. Liam was just one of those guys who got better every day.

"That's what happens in small towns, love. Just one three-way call is all it takes." He got out of the car, then made his way to her side. He opened the door and reached for her hand.

Before her heeled foot touched the ground, a camera was in her face and a microphone was hanging over her head. She pressed her lips together, trying to pretend she wasn't on film. She had to act natural, but it was hard. Since they'd come in a separate town car, she'd forgotten about the cameramen and boom men being sent ahead with them. "Thanks," she said to Liam, then stood. She looked up at him, loving his model-tall height, then turned and peered at the hotel. She nodded and smiled. "You're right. The hotel is quaint." Her eyes moved to the camera crew. She still didn't understand why they had to capture everything. Their rooms had never been televised, and neither had their arrival. She shrugged. It was what it was, and she'd asked for it, she reminded herself.

"Charly! Over here," someone said, speed walking toward her, holding a cell phone in an outstretched hand.

"Oh, yes. Liam! Liam, please speak for us? Say anything. I just wanna hear your accent," a woman, who looked old enough to be their mom, yelled as part of the group made their way down the block toward them.

"Well?" Liam asked, still holding Charly's hand. "Shall we run for it?" he teased.

Charly smiled, waving to the group that was now only feet from them. "The show has begun," she said through clenched teeth.

"It's your baby," he reminded her, then cut his eyes to the right.

A young lady stood there wearing a morbid look that belonged on a corpse in a coffin, and was uniformed in a black suit, minus the jacket. The rest of her looked like a hodgepodge of stages and ages had exploded on her. Her eyes looked like they'd been borrowed from the eighties, complete with tons of blue and black liner. She had a crystal in the middle of her forehead like she hailed from India, and she had fire-engine-red locks coiled around the sides of her head, tied in a back knot. Her name tag read HEAVEN. "Welcome to Tallulahville, Ms. St. James and Mr. Liam. We've been expecting you. I'm Heaven, and I'll be assisting you with your bags," she said dryly, not even the least bit interested in inquiring about Liam's last name, then rolled a brass luggage cart toward the trunk.

Charly's eyes bulged. "A bell*girl?* Cool. I've never met one before. I like that, and I like your name." Charly's greeting was genuine.

Heaven spread her lips, but didn't smile. She had a gap in the center of her row of top teeth. "Thanks, and thanks," she said, nodding, then tried to make her way to the trunk.

Liam stuck out his arm, blocking the luggage cart. "Though I respect what you do, I'm afraid I can't stand here and watch you get our bags. Any gentleman would-n't." He reached into his pocket, took out some money, and pressed it into her hand. He shook his head, then nodded toward the driver and asked him to put the bags on the cart. "Heaven, please tell the front desk I don't want the bags in the rooms just yet, and I'd appreciate them holding them behind the counter."

Heaven heaved and rolled her eyes. "Okay. So . . . would that be just *your* bags? You did say I, not we." She shook her head and tsked a little. "Don't get me wrong. I'm not slow or anything, but in the hospitality business you have to be specific. Customer service is key . . . that's what they've stressed to me each time I've been sus-pended for not catering." She shrugged. "So, are we just holding your bags or both of you guys'? And who takes the blame? 'Cause I'm not."

Liam smiled. "I like you, Heaven. You're professional and sweet. I can't imagine why anyone would suspend you for lack of catering," he said sarcastically, laughing a little. Heaven didn't join him; she just stood there. Charly's brows shot up. "You can just have them hold *all* of our luggage—mine and Charly's," he said, then looked at Charly. "And you can blame it on Charly's assistant." His eyes moved away, and a smile stretched wide. "Charly, here they are," he announced when the group of people who'd been calling them finally reached them. "You can work this one out. Dealing with Heaven drained me enough. I'm done working for today."

Charly waved a fake good-bye to Heaven, who'd already begun to walk off, then smirked at Liam. She thrust her laptop carrier into his chest. "You wish. You are working, assistant. Hold my bag," she said as low as she could, her eyes moving across the faces of the group. She nodded to them all, then began shaking hands, and signing autographs as she made small talk.

"Here, Charly. Here!" the girl with the cell phone said, thrusting it into her face. "Rory wants you. She couldn't make it here, so she sent me. I'm Kat, her sister," she said in one breath, handing the phone to Charly.

Charly smiled, then took the phone. She needed to talk to Rory to get the dish on Nia. "Rory, nice to talk to you," she said.

"What it tiz, Charly, my girl? Sorry I couldn't make it down to meet you, but you know how it is. A sista has things to do, people to see, places to go. I'm tryna get my money up 'cause I gotta get a new celly to replace this dime store phone I got." Rory greeted her like she and Charly were old friends, and rambled on and on about having a cheap cell phone. Charly almost cringed. Rory's voice wasn't just high-pitched, it was squeaky.

Charly nodded, not knowing how to respond. Rory was clearly different.

"Yo, Charly! You there, sis?" Rory asked. "This stupid dime store phone!"

"Rory? Rory? Can you hear me? I'm here, and I can hear you," Charly said, holding the phone close to her ear and tilting her head.

"Yeah, sis. I got'cha now. I got everything you need. Trust me, there's nothing or no one I don't know. You can just call me the map and keys to Tallulahville. That said, what's up, sis? What it tiz? I've been blowing my cool waiting to talk to you. I didn't know we'd be working one on one when I nominated my girl, Nia. But I'm glad for the connect. 'Nah mean?"

Charly's eyebrows shot north. She had a live one on her hands, but she could handle it. She'd had plenty of experience with the street, and knew how to converse with all sorts of people. "Yes, Rory. I know what you mean. It's nice talking to you too, and we need to get together soon. I really need to speak to you," she said, then threw Liam an extrapleasant look and huge phony smile, hoping he'd catch that conversing with Rory was a struggle.

"Sure sis, sure. I got'cha. We need to chop it up. That ain't no thang. It's not like a sista got a lot goings on. I'm just over here chillin' at the love nest." Rory's explanation was contradictory. Only seconds ago she'd said she was too busy to go anywhere.

Had Rory really just said "goings on"? Charly questioned. And what and where exactly was the love nest? "I'm sorry, what did you say? You don't have a lot to do today, and you're where . . . at a nest?" she asked, hoping Rory would repeat herself.

"To the first question, I'm at the love nest. Ya know, the crib. I'm over here getting my pretty on. And to your second question, it's not like I got a lot goings on. I just need to get my feet did," Rory answered, matter-of-factly, clearly not realizing she'd mixed up Charly's inquiries.

Charly giggled quietly, then listened as Rory rattled on and on, sounding more uneducated by the second. Before long, she couldn't hold her composure. "Here. Here," she said. "Please give my assistant your number, and I'll call you later." She thrust the phone at Liam.

"Me?" he questioned, then rolled his eyes. "You're taking this assistant thing too far. Pass me your phone so I can lock her number in," he said, then took the call and Charly's cell. He logged Rory's number into Charly's phone book, thanked her, then ended the call. He handed the phone back to its owner, and they both bid her good-bye.

"Whew, that one's a piece of work," Charly began, still laughing.

Liam elbowed her sharply. "Look," he said in a loud whisper. His head nodded toward the sidewalk. "Seems your folder contents are wrong. No tools needed."

Charly looked over to the walk. Her eyebrows rose. "What in the—"

"Heck," Liam said, saving her from cursing. "That has to be her."

A girl who looked like Nia walked by them, her head held high. She was surrounded by a few hot guys, who were apparently trying to get at her. Her heart-shaped face was pretty, flanked by shoulder-length black tresses. Her expression was happy, and she was trendily dressed. Charly shook her head. Her mission was failing before she could even start. Charly apologized to the group, then about-faced, making her way to the car. "Liam!" she yelled, then waved her hands to the cameraman and boom guy. "Let's go."

"Where are you going, Charly?" Liam asked, making his way to her while the two-man camera crew ran to keep up. "We gotta check in to the hotel, scout stores, stay on time and within budget. You know how it goes, and—"

"No, and nope. I'm working on a wish factor—I *wish* I would be stupid enough to just follow the schedule. Didn't you just see her? I'm getting down to the bottom of this. Get in the car. I'm calling Rory back, and we're going to the real source. The mayor's house."

3

The car pulled into a long drive that had perfectly manicured bushes lining it, and Charly's jaw dropped. Suddenly it was if they were in another world. A huge house met her eyes. It was beautiful in every sense of the word, sitting on top of a small hill. *Majestic* was the only word she could think of to describe it. Charly turned her attention back to her conversation.

"Day, I'm telling you there's a problem," she said, cutting Mr. Day's name in half. Her phone began making weird noises, forcing her to look at the screen. Her reception was dwindling, she noticed as her bars began to disappear. "We saw Nia. Well, it looked just like Nia. And we've been duped, and I'm not standing for it."

"Charly! Charly? Can you hear me? Look at the folder—" was all Charly could make out before the call dropped. She looked at her screen again. NO SERVICE replaced her reception bars and 4G status. She tossed the phone on the seat, irritated. The same thing happened when she'd called Rory, and she'd thought it was Rory's dime store phone. She needed reception now more than ever.

"Well, love? What did he say?" Liam asked, picking up her phone. He looked at hers, then at his. "Mine is dead, too."

The car pulled up in front of the house, and Charly's eyes stretched wider. Expensive cars lined the drive and were in the four-car garage that stood as tall as the house. Its doors were opened, and a young guy was inside wiping down the automobiles.

"Uh, is he like a driver?" she asked, now more peeved than ever. First it was the lie about Nia being dowdy, and now they'd been sent to help a family who, obviously, weren't strapped for cash. "What's the point? I thought we were here to help someone who can't help themselves. It looks like they can write a check to fix everything."

"No wonder the mayor decided to work out of his home in the interim," Liam said, then opened his car door. He got out, then made his way over to Charly's side, opening her door for her. He scratched his head, then licked his lips. "Calm down, Charly. The mission is still the mission. We didn't specify an income bracket, and the last time I checked, teenagers don't have money, their parents do."

Charly got out, then looked around. She tossed her hair, slid on her sunglasses, and puffed her attitude. She wasn't one to fall for the okeydoke, and she wouldn't start now. She wanted answers, and someone was going to give them.

"Hello and welcome." An older gentleman walked out of the house and down the short walk to meet them. "Charly and Liam, I suppose."

"Check yourself, Charly. Don't snap. There has to be a reason behind all this, just as this guy has to be the mayor. He looks political," Liam whispered to her through clenched teeth and a pasted-on smile.

Charly flung her hair again, trying to quiet her emotions, but it was hard. Her attitude had an attitude, and she didn't know if she could check two of them. She bit her lip, adjusted her shades, then made herself act like she was happy. The corners of her mouth spread into a wide smile, and she proffered her hand to the mayor. "Thank you for having us," she greeted. "Can you show us around? I'd love to see the place and get a feel for our mission," she said.

Liam patted her back like a proud father. "Yes, that'd be great," he agreed.

The mayor nodded, knowingly. "Sure. I'll have someone show you around for the *mission*," he said with emphasis, winking. "Also, you'll have to forgive me. The date must've been logged into my calendar wrong. I wasn't expecting you until tomorrow, so I was just headed out for a meeting. I must take care of the town you know. That's priority," he spoke directly into the camera.

Well, that's cheesy, she thought. "I understand, Mr. Mayor. My priority is to take care of your daughter. Speaking of your daughter, I think there's been a mistake," she began, then felt Liam's foot press down on hers.

"Yes, we've got work to do. And I have the greatest

confidence in you," the mayor said, obviously missing Charly's statement. "You know I'm a fan of the show. It took a different tone when you became the main female host," he complimented.

Charly knew his last statement would be edited out because it could be taken as a low blow to the show's concept, which was supposed to be the focus, not the cast. Still, though, she appreciated it. She smiled hard, this time genuine. The mayor was playing it up for the audience, but she didn't expect anything less. He was a politician, after all. She looked around for a second, taking the property in. She wasn't sure what a mayor's income was, but from the looks of things, he wasn't only a government official, he was probably the richest man in town. She turned back to him when something caught her eye. There was someone watching them through the upstairs window. Charly shielded her eyes from the sun to get a better glimpse. A female figure stood in the window, but Charly couldn't make her out. She couldn't tell if the person was young or old or, as she zeroed in more, if she was a she at all. The figure was just too far away for Charly to tell. "Thank you, sir. But about the mission, do you have a sec?"

"I'm afraid not, but we'll talk later." He extended his hand to her, then turned to Liam.

A car breezed up the drive from behind, its music blasting from inside. Charly shook the mayor's hand, trying to ignore the person in the window and the approaching car, but it was hard. The person in the window seemed to move, and the music's bass was heavy, the vibration sounded in the air, overpowering whatever the

mayor was saying to Liam. A Rick Ross remix was playing when the car parked.

The mayor stopped talking, focusing on the car. The
passenger door opened, and his lips spread into a smile
so warm and loving that everything seemed to go quiet,
even the music. "Mya! There you are," he said.

"Mya?" Liam asked in a loud whisper.

Hands set shopping bags on the ground, then a lone high-
heeled strappy sandaled foot met the blacktopped drive
from behind the opened car door. "Daddy!" a singsong
voice called out, followed by a girl with a pretty heart-
shaped face, flanked by shoulder-length black tresses. Her
strappy sandals were killer hot, and the rest of her was
trendy.

"Mya!" He turned to Charly and Liam. "My daughter," he informed.

Her, Charly thought, her eyes meeting the girl she and
Liam had seen near their hotel. "Mya, not Nia?" she
questioned aloud before she knew it. Quickly, she'd
pulled out the folder, and began flipping through it. She
didn't know how she missed a main detail. Nia was an
identical twin. Immediately, she turned back toward the
house, her eyes searching the window to see the person
who stood behind it, but it was too late. The curtains
swished, revealing no one. From the sudden movement of
the window treatments, Charly could tell that whoever it
was had just walked away, and she'd bet a dollar to a
dime it was Nia.

Liam cleared his throat, and Charly looked at him. His
eyes held interest, but she couldn't tell what kind. She
turned to Mya, taking her in. Yes, she was much prettier

than the pictures of Nia, but she wasn't pretty enough to capture Liam's attention, not in a I-wanna-get-to-know-you way. Charly elbowed him. "Well, well, well. It looks like you may still need my tools," he said, laughing. He turned to her, raised his eyebrows, then exhaled loudly, silently asking her to follow his example.

Charly breathed, then grinned. She had indeed been holding her breath, a habit she'd developed recently, she noted.

"Ah, it's you." A voice pulled her attention from Liam. A singsong tone that belonged to Mya.

Charly turned her head and looked into Mya's expressive eyes. Her irises seemed to dance, and her teeth gleamed. She would've been a perfect toothpaste commercial candidate. She nodded, not knowing how else to respond. She was relieved that Mya wasn't Nia, but there was something that she was missing. Even with Mya's singsong voice, twinkling eyes, and beautiful teeth, something seemed empty, missing. *Phony?* "Yes, it's me." Charly proffered her hand to Mya. "Nice to meet you, Mya. I'm Charly."

Mya nodded. "With a y. I know." Her head turned to Liam, and she held him with a gaze for seconds before she spoke. "And you're Liam. Are you going to renovate my space too?" she asked, making Charly want to kick her. She'd put on an innocent face and tone, but Charly recognize a flirt when she heard one, and since the world thought that she and Liam were an item, she felt disrespected.

Charly stepped in front of Liam as leisurely as she

could without being obvious. "Afraid not, Mya. Our mission is your father's office, and Liam . . . he's my mission man," she sang, then turned to the mayor. "Can we go in now?"

The mayor nodded, bid everyone good-bye, then made his way over to one of the cars. He paused. "Take your time, Charly and Liam. The mission you speak of will require a lot of work . . . not in my opinion though. I'm just stating other people's facts," he said, then got in the car and closed the door.

Charly looked at Liam with raised brows. She couldn't believe what had come out of the mayor's mouth, but it did. She didn't care how he'd dressed up the statement, it was low. "All righty then, Liam. Let's do it."

"Yes, let's do it, Liam," Mya said, making her way to the house with bags in her hand she'd managed to retrieve without Charly noticing. "Follow me," she instructed.

Charly stepped inside and blinked rapidly. Her eyes had to be deceiving her. She looked at Liam, who shrugged, then turned and looked into the living room that was situated to the right of the foyer. MYA FOR PROM QUEEN signs were everywhere, and there had to be at least a hundred or more, Charly guessed, taking in the colors and Mya's photo on each one. She turned back around, eyeing the walls of the foyer and the library, which was on the other side. Portraits of Mya lined the walls, and a huge oil painting of her hung dead center on the main one as if Mya were royalty. Charly walked around the space, taking in each picture. Surely there had to be at least one of Nia.

"Wow, summer just began. Getting ready for prom almost a year early?" Liam asked, a bit of a chuckle in his throat.

Mya smiled. "You can never be too prepared . . . especially, when it's expected of you," she said. Liam raised his brows in question. "You know, as head cheerleader and homecoming queen and mayor's daughter, prom queen is like my rite of passage," she said, owning her privileges without remorse or apology.

"So you're an only child. It must be nice," Charly said, hoping Mya would bite. She wasn't sure if Mya knew the real reason she and Liam were there or not, or if she'd heard her mention Nia's name outside, so she decided to test it.

"Most of the time," Mya said matter-of-factly, moving her hair out of her eyes. "I have a sister, but she doesn't like pictures or people or popularity, just calculus, chemistry, and colleges—just like the colleges like her since she aced her pre-SATs two years before she had to take them. Boring stuff." She shook her head. "Which is too bad—for me and for her. It makes me always have to be the one out front. That's hard work." She flashed a smile, then killed it, making Charly question if it were genuine or not. "If you go down that hall, and turn left, you can go through the kitchen to get to my dad's outside office. It's just right off the pool house. You can't miss it. I'd take you, but I have to get ready for a party tonight. My ride will be here before I know it, and being fashionably late may work for parties, but not rides." She looked at Liam and pointed. "And you . . ." she began, then wagged her index finger at him and Charly. "I mean, you two can come if you want."

Charly shook her head, passing up the opportunity for them both. "Next time. Are you sure you don't have time to show us out? I really don't like walking around peoples' houses."

Mya shook her head. "Not my area," she said, shrugging. "Sorry."

Charly huffed. "And what does that mean? *Not your area?*" She tilted her head. "We're here to help *your* family, and you say it's not your area? Are you out of your—"

"Good enough, then," Liam said, interrupting. "We'll find our way."

Mya gulped. "I'm not being rude. I'm just doing as I was told by my dad."

"Whatever," Charly said, then grabbed Liam by the hand, and headed down the hall.

By the time they made it to the office that was adjacent to the pool house, someone was in a window again, and Charly wondered if it were Nia, then changed her mind. Whoever it was had blondish hair, a shade Nia didn't have. She flipped through the folder she had on her to be sure, then shook her head. According to the data the studio had collected on Nia, Nia was all natural. Because she sat holed up in her room, her watching from windows didn't match her personality. It'd been reported that she lived most of life behind her closed bedroom door, only leaving when she had to. The girl was clearly depressed. It didn't take a psychiatrist to figure that one out, Charly thought. She pressed her lips together, wondering who it was that kept watching them.

The water glimmered under the sun, the slight breeze making it wave. Liam shook the office's door handle, then exhaled. "It's locked."

Charly looked around, admiring the Olympic-sized pool surrounded by flagstone and lush greenery, then smiled, noticing an outdoor kitchen. A real bar set on one side of the pool, and what appeared to be an entertainment station was on the other. "Liam, this isn't a backyard, it's an oasis." Her eyes moved from the beautiful space up to the window again and met swinging curtains, an indication of someone being there seconds before. "Are you sure it's locked?" she asked.

Liam shook it again. "Yep. But there's a keypad here. Look in the folder and see if you have the code."

"It's 6446246," a girl's voice said from behind, making both Charly and Liam jump.

Charly turned and faced her mission. Ms. Nia, in the flesh, sporting an awful camel-colored hair bonnet. A head covering that resembled the blondish hair color Charly saw in the window. So Nia had been watching.

4

Nia's face was a battleground. A jagged scar was on one cheek, and the other was an area marked in defeat. Her brows were worse in person than in the photos. Bushy and low, they looked as if they were grown to shield the suffering behind them. If she had any inner beauty, one would have to have X-ray vision to see it. Her look was that bleak. Charly smiled, trying not to stare at the zigzag on Nia's skin, and took note that it had healed nicely. It wasn't appealing, but it wasn't a keloid, which meant that makeup could cover the line of demarcation. "Oh, you must be Nia," Charly said, then could've kicked herself. She was sure she wasn't supposed to know who Nia was. The whole makeover was supposed to seem to happen by mistake. She'd been told that was the only way the girl would go for it. But even the studio had to allow for the cast to know about the people in the house they were going to make over, she assured herself. So it was no big deal.

"Or are you Mya?" Liam asked, lying and saving Charly. "Your father just told us he had two daughters. Twins, right?"

Nia nodded, offering what Charly assumed was her version of a closed-mouth smile. The corners of her lips didn't rise, but she'd pressed them together. At least she'd made an effort, Charly thought. "The code is 6446246," she repeated.

Liam raised his brows. "Oh, sorry. I forgot." He pressed the keypad seven times, and a beep sounded.

"I think that should be everything you need," Nia said, then turned to walk away.

Charly gulped. This girl was going to be harder to work with than she thought. She had to come up with something to keep her around and quick. Liam stretched his eyes, urging her on. Charly shrugged. "Uh, Nia? Wait. Don't leave!"

Nia turned around. Her look hadn't changed, and Charly was sure there had to be corpses with more expression. Her eyes asked what Charly wanted, and her mouth said nothing.

Charly walked over to her. "I don't mean to intrude, but I do need some help. I don't know my way around, and I need to get some things for the show. My bags . . ." She shrugged, trying to think of a way to fluff a lie. "They didn't come in yet, and I have to have something to wear. What size are you?"

Nia gave herself a once-over. "I'm bigger than you. I wear a nine in clothes, size seven shoes. But I'm afraid you're talking to the wrong sister. Mya's the shopper," she deadpanned.

Charly leaned closer to her, and masked her face with an uncomfortable look. "It's not necessarily the clothes I'm worried about, though I do need them. It's my toiletries. You know, girl stuff?" As soon as the words came out, she knew she'd said the wrong thing. She was at a house with two teenaged girls. Of course they had to have feminine items.

Nia gave Charly a duh look. "That's easy. Come on," she said, then beckoned for Charly to follow her.

"I'll be back," Charly told Liam. When Nia's back was turned, Liam gave Charly a thumbs-up. "Nia, I really appreciate you helping me. It's kinda hard to get the things I need when all I have around me are guys. If you know what I mean," she said, following Nia into the house.

Nia only nodded, then led the way through the butler pantry, kitchen, then finally to a back staircase Charly hadn't seen. They continued to walk in silence, and Charly pushed her mind to come up with something to help her connect with the girl. She was so drawn in, and wouldn't seem to allow Charly to get close to her. Charly wondered why Nia was so emotionally distant as she stepped onto a landing, then looked around. There were only a couple of doors in the hall, definitely not enough to house all the bedrooms needed for the family members.

"Since there are only three doors, and that one is clearly a bathroom, I assume your house is set up in wings," Charly said, pointing to the open rest room door.

"Presume," Nia corrected. "Assume is when you're not sure of something, like a complete guess. When you're guessing based on irrefutable evidence—like three doors and one being a bathroom—the word is *presume.* Assume and presume both mean the same thing; however, they're used based on what's known and what's just a guess," Nia said, looking at Charly. She turned her head back around, then headed to the closed door at the end of the hall. "And yes, you're right. This is the teen wing. My parents' wing is off of another staircase." She opened the door, then beckoned Charly to follow.

Nia's life definitely enabled her nonsocial behavior, Charly noticed, when Nia only walked steps from the bedroom door and turned into an en suite bathroom. With only seconds of time to take it all in, Charly saw that Nia pretty much had everything she needed in the space, except the full-fledged library and science lab Liam and the crew would build. In one sweep of the eye she saw a bed, computer, tons of books, and a mini fridge, and nothing was out of place. In fact, the place was so neat it resembled a magazine picture. Charly shuddered. She wondered if antisocial behavior, depression, and a case of the blahs were all Nia had, because, from the looks of things, she could've been a candidate for obsessive compulsive disorder, too. Teens just weren't supposed to be so clean, not to the point where there wasn't even a wrinkle on the bedspread.

"In here," Nia said, holding open the door to a linen closet. "Middle shelf." She pointed, then walked away, right past Charly, then made her way back into her bedroom.

Charly heard a chair roll across the floor, then walked

over to the linen closet. She leaned in a little, then moved things around. She didn't need feminine products, but she had to play the part if she wanted to be convincing. In seconds, she'd retrieved her cell phone from her pocket and held it up, hoping the signal had strengthened. She nodded when she saw the bars had risen a bit, then opened the Web app. She began Googling pharmacies in the small town. There was a major one and one she assumed was a mom-and-pop. She did a search for another big-brand pharmacy, hoping like crazy there wasn't one too near. She had to get Nia out of her comfort zone and into hers. *Please. Please. Please*, Charly begged, *let there be one by a mall. Any mall.* Being from the Midwest, she knew that even small towns had nearby malls, even if they were located in a different centrally placed small town. "Yes!" she accidently whispered when a major pharmacy popped up by a shopping center. "Nia, can you come here?" she called, tucking her phone back into her pocket, then bending her head as if she were really looking for something in the linen closet. The chair rolled again.

"Yes," Nia said, from the doorway seconds later.

Charly shook her head. "I'm afraid I can't use any of this stuff." She turned to look at Nia, and tried to focus on her eyes. Between the jagged scar and awful bonnet on her head, Charly had a hard time zeroing in where she was supposed to. She didn't want to offend her, sure many stared at the mark on her face, so she concentrated on the space between her eyebrows.

Nia barely stretched her eyes in wonder, but Charly

could tell she'd piqued her interest. "Mya may have what you need. We're identical by DNA only, but that's where it stops. She may have other brands or types."

Charly grimaced, then shrugged. "I don't think so. Unless she gets a prescription, I don't think anything she has will work. My body and skin are hypersensitive, so I'm limited to what my dermatologist prescribes. I don't know what I was thinking . . . I guess I wasn't. Sorry to waste your time." Charly whipped out her cell, then started swiping the screen. She smiled. She was the actress of the year, she told herself. She didn't know how she came up with such believable tales, but was glad. "Ah-ha! We're in business." She pretended to read an e-mail. "My doctor called in a prescription to the pharmacy. Can you take me to CVS, the one by the mall? That's the one I told them about."

Nia shook her head, and her eyes seemed to brighten. "There's no CVS by the mall."

"Walgreens, then?" Charly said, correcting her lie. She'd been so focused on the mall, she'd forgotten what she'd just read. She'd traveled a lot with the show, and no matter where the cast was she'd spotted one of the two pharmacies, if not both.

Nia's face changed back into defeat. She nodded. "Yes, *Walgreens.* I don't know, Charly. I'm working on a big research project . . . If I go anywhere, I'm going to the library."

Charly wasn't going to let Nia get away so easily. It was summertime, so whatever project she was working on, if she was really working on anything, could wait. It had to. She had a mission to accomplish, and she wasn't going to let Nia or anyone else stop her. "Please, Nia. I'll owe you one. It's just that . . ." She shrugged, then made herself look sad. "No one gets me. The studio dresses me up, and I'm on TV, and I get to do a lot of great things. From the outside I know it looks like I've got it made, but it's been a trying journey," she said truthfully. "But, honestly, no one's ever understood me." She fluffed her lie again, hoping she could make Nia empathize. "I don't know if you understand what that's like—to not have anyone really get you."

Nia pressed her lips together and blinked really slowly. Her inhale and exhale were audible and almost seemed deliberate. Yes, everyone had to breathe, Charly knew, but no one had to do it so loudly. Nia cleared her throat.

"Do you know what that's like, Nia?" Charly pushed, hoping for a sign, any slight change on Nia's face that would be a telltale sign that she was biting.

Nia pursed her lips, then looked to the ceiling like she was searching for an answer. Or remembering, Charly thought. She'd once read somewhere that people looked up and to the left or right, depending if they were recalling or making up something. She hoped Nia was in memory mode.

"I don't know . . ." Nia said. "Maybe you can talk to Mya."

Charly stopped herself from shrugging. At this point she didn't care what Nia thought she didn't know. If she was going to remake this girl, she had to find a way to make Nia help her do so. She looked at her, seeing that Nia was really into working and studying. Her whole look said nerd, but it didn't scream it like it should've.

Charly figured if Nia wanted to be nerdy, she should be the best at it. And that's just what Charly would assist her in doing. "Okay, let me know," she said, then walked around Nia and went straight into her bedroom. Her eyes scanned the space, and somehow it appeared even cleaner than it had seconds before. "What's all this stuff you read?" she asked, walking toward the floor-to-ceiling bookshelf. She reached out, touching the spines of all the hardcovers, looking for something recognizable when a slither of something red with white lettering caught her attention.

"Science and math, mostly," Nia was saying as she made it into the bedroom portion of the suite, then made her way over to where Charly was. She reached out, and swiped whatever the red thing was, then tucked it into her pocket.

Charly looked over her shoulder and saw Nia's discomfort. The girl clearly didn't like her things touched. Charly cocked her head and lifted her brows. "Is that jazz or classical music?" she asked, trying to identify what was playing. It was hard to tell because it was so low.

"No. It's not music. It's vibrations. They help with comprehension and retention. I don't listen to music."

Charly thought she was going to die. There couldn't be any way possible that everyone didn't listen to music. "Really?" she asked, walking over to the docking system where the MP3 was, and was glad they had something in common, which would help her. Charly removed Nia's iPod, selected the orange music button on her phone, docked her cell and turned up the volume. Suddenly a Rihanna song blasted through the speakers. "Not even this?" Charly yelled, bopping her head, and walking away to touch other things in the room. Items she hoped would make Nia uncomfortable.

"What are you doing?" Nia snapped, turning down the music.

Charly walked to the other wall, and looked at the framed pictures that sat on top of a smaller bookcase. She nodded, noticing one of Nia and some girl she seemed to be chummy with, in what had to be their younger years. She smiled a bit, thankful that Nia had at least one friend, then picked it up and looked at Nia. "Who's this? Your friend?"

Nia shot Charly a nasty glare and nodded. "Kind of," she began, then seemed to catch herself. Her mean look was quickly replaced by a bland one. "But then again, Rory is everyone's friend. Everyone in my house, that is. She's cool," she answered as if talking were painful.

Charly raised her brows, wondering if Nia was really shy and depressed like everyone thought she was or if she was just undercover with her meanness. Her attitude had just flip-flopped, which made Charly question Nia's true character. Charly averted her eyes to the photo and studied it. *So this is Rory?* she thought, now able to marry a face with the girl she'd spoken to on the cell earlier. She looked over at Nia again, noticing how perplexed she looked. She was trying Nia's patience, and she knew it. She set the frame back on top of the shelf, squatted down, then finger-walked through the books until she saw one she wanted. She selected an old yearbook, walked back over to the docked iPhone, turned up the music again, then hopped on Nia's bed. She put up her feet, then opened the hardcover, looking for Nia's picture. "Oh. This is you?" she asked, locating Nia quicker than she'd thought she would. She flipped the yearbook around in her hand, turning the open page to face Nia.

Nia shook her head. "Mya, in chemistry class," she mouthed, then removed Charly's phone from the docking device. "Chemistry was her subject for a while thanks to our dad."

"Your dad? I don't understand," Charly said, looking at Nia for an explanation.

Nia shrugged. "It's simple really. Since we're twins, our parents divvied us up so we wouldn't feel cheated of attention. My dad focuses on Mya, my mom focuses on me, so, in a way, we're pretty close to having the lives of only children—I guess. Both of them parent us though."

Charly nodded, then flipped the book back over, and gulped. Mya and Nia had been identical in every sense of the word before: bad hair, worse clothes, and all. She turned the page until she got to their individual student pictures, then noticed that Nia didn't have a scar then. She wondered what happened. What had made Mya transform into one of the beautiful ones, and Nia delve deeper into Yuckdom? She closed the cover partway and looked at the year. It had only been a couple of years ago. "So when did you—"

Nia took the yearbook from Charly, and put it back in the bookcase. "Don't you have to go to the pharmacy? I thought that was so important."

"See. I thought you'd understand," Charly said, smiling. She was glad her plan to drive Nia batty enough to make her want out of her space had worked. "I knew you were the only one I could ask to do this favor for me." She got off the bed. "You'll take me then, right? Otherwise, I'm stuck here until"—she shrugged—"who knows?"

"Okay, Charly." Nia caved, grabbing an awful-looking purse from the desk chair, then took out keys. "You're difficult," she said, a slight smile parting her lips.

Charly breezed past her, snatching off the camel-colored bonnet, then headed to the bedroom door and opened it. She shrugged. "Sorry, I couldn't help it. That bonnet's been killing me since I saw it, and, trust me, it's been killing you too. You just don't know it," she said, looking over her shoulder, her hand still on the knob. "And I've heard that I'm difficult a lot." Nia's smile grew wider, then her eyes lit. She reached up and touched her now-exposed dusty-looking brown hair, and slid her hands over it, smoothing out a ponytail. Charly didn't think her statement warranted that much glee. She knew she was right when she realized Nia's focus and grin wasn't for her, but were directed past her. She turned back around, and almost jumped. A guy was standing in the hallway, and she hadn't heard him approach.

"Hi," he said, first looking directly at Charly, then he glanced at Nia, giving her a quick wave and an even quicker half-grin that bordered on politeness, not want. He turned his attention back to Charly, smiling whole-heartedly. "I heard you guys were going to make over the mayor's office. I just wanted to see if there was anything I can do. I can help with the set."

Charly quickly looked over her shoulder again, and saw that Nia's face still held interest. She turned to the guy and sized him up with one indifferent swoop of the eyes. He was average height, had a fresh haircut, a brilliant smile, and that was it. There was nothing about him that screamed hot boy or remarkable. His looks, style, and magnetism scored a whopping zilch to Liam's off-the-charts record of extraordinary fineness. She shrugged. She just didn't get what was so magnificent about him that was obviously attracting Nia. She beckoned Nia to come closer. "I'm not sure. Nia, what do you think?" she asked, when Nia was by her side. "Can the show use . . . What's your name?"

"Trent. The name's Trent," he told her with a smile. "Nia can tell you I'm a good guy. I can be pretty handy."

Charly looked at Nia for confirmation, then paused. In less than a second Nia's smile flatlined. Quickly, she turned back to Trent to see what had happened, and she locked eyes with Mya, who had somehow made her way in front of him.

"Oh, it looks like you're going somewhere," Mya said. A smile was pasted on her face while she nodded toward Nia and the keys she had in hand. "I wanna roll."

Charly ping-ponged her eyes between the sisters, and she could tell from Nia's expression that Mya tagging along wouldn't be good for her plan. She didn't know what the tension was between the sisters, but she could feel it, just as she knew she'd get to the bottom of it. "Maybe next time? The cameramen will have to ride, so there won't be any room because of their equipment," she kind of lied. Yes, they'd be following, that she was sure of, but they'd be in a separate car.

5

Charly ran into the pharmacy, headed straight to the candy aisle, selected a pack of gum, then made her way to where the stationery was located. She needed to buy time and, also, a notebook. She'd taken up the habit of taking pictures of all the shots she wanted to remember, but she couldn't bring herself to use the Notes app in her phone to recall words. Putting pen to paper just felt better to her. Ever since the last English class she'd taken, she couldn't help it. There she'd learned more than words and proper verses improper use, and how much of an educated crab her teacher had been. She'd been taught the art of note taking and how writing things down helped her to remember. This time, she needed to keep track of her to-do and must-do lists, and conceive of a way to accomplish getting everything done for Nia. That would require sketching a hierarchy. She had to start with imagining the finished product, and then work backward from there to accomplish it, she decided, not letting herself be wooed by the dozens of notebooks in front of her, tempting her with color or design. She shrugged and picked out one small enough that she could carry in her bag, and headed to the checkout. She whipped out her phone while she was standing in line and scrolled through her contacts.

"Rory? This is Charly," she said, after dialing. "I need you. Where are you?" She moved up as the line shortened to just one person in front of her.

"Sista. Sista. Sista. A sista's in East Jesus, right now," Rory said, with noise clanking in the background.

Charly reared back her head in wonder and walked in front of the cashier. She put her items on the counter, then covered the phone. "Excuse me, miss?" she asked the older woman, who looked to be in her sixties. "Can you please tell me how to get to East Jesus? How far is it from here?"

The cashier, who'd already begun to ring up Charly's gum and notebook, looked at her like she was Satan himself. "East Jesus?" She fingered a cross on her neck. "You tryna be funny, child?"

Charly shook her head, then looked at her watch. She'd been in the pharmacy at least five minutes, which was enough time for her plan, she thought. "No, ma'am, one second." She turned her attention back to her phone. "Rory, you did say you were in East Jesus, right? Where's that?"

Rory started laughing. "Girl, East Jesus ain't a real place. It means I'm out in the middle of nowhere. Unless you gonna come scoop me, I won't be back until tomorrow, I guess."

Charly apologized to the cashier, told Rory to text her the address, and disconnected the call. She paid for her stuff, took her bag, then sped out of the automatic door. Rory wasn't any help, she realized, when she'd jogged to the car and hopped in. "Sorry, it's not ready yet," she lied to Nia. "Seems there must've been other prescriptions called or brought in or something. They said it could be at least an hour." She reached into the bag and pulled out the gum. "Have some?"

Nia shook her head. "An hour? I don't know, Charly. I have so much to do."

Charly snapped her fingers as if she just had a thought. "Research, right? Well, there's a mall right there, so there has to be a bookstore in there, right? You said you need to go to the library."

Nia exhaled, then drummed her hands on the steering wheel. "No, I said if I had to go anywhere, it'd be the library."

Charly laughed. "Same difference. Let's go. I need to check out some design ideas anyway. I can check out a couple of magazines while you get your books." She looked at Nia, then pouted. "C'mon, Nia. I never get to hang out with just girls. It'll be my treat. I get a nice per diem," she said, teasing and elbowing Nia as if she could really impress her with her daily allowance, as she liked to refer to the daily spending and living money the studio gave her while she was touring with the show. "C'mon. C'mon. C'mon," she pushed until Nia gave in.

* * *

Teenagers were everywhere. Every single place her eyes could see, another one popped up. Charly shook her head. The town was so small, she couldn't understand the mathematics. The ratio of teens to adults made no sense. She took Nia's arm in her hand, and the two of them made their way through the local mall, stopping every so often to look through store windows. Charly grabbed her cell, held it up to a store sign, then took a picture. That's how she kept up with things now; she snapped shots.

"Well?" Nia asked. "Maybe we should just head straight to the bookstore so you can look at magazines. I doubt if anything else in here will pique your interest."

Charly shook her head. "First, let me see if anything pops into my mind. It may be something that triggers my designer side. This is for your dad, remember? Help a sista out, Nia." She laughed, and was glad to hear Nia join her.

They walked another hundred feet or so. "Well, anything you can work with yet? There's not much. It's just the usual department store and cheesy fashion stores that cater to allowance budgets. I think it's all atrocious—the shopping. I just don't get what's so important about clothes."

Charly grunted, then slyly took in Nia's outfit, wondering how dare the girl call anything atrocious. What she was wearing had died and been buried seasons ago, and she had the nerve to still rock it. Bootcut jeans flared over her outdated sneakers, and a no-name ill-fitted shirt hid her upper torso. Charly did everything she could not to roll her eyes. Nia's drab ponytail should've been covered by a hat or garbage bag. "We're gonna have to make time to go into Minneapolis." She swiped her phone screen, then pulled up her e-mail. I had one of the studio girls send an alternative list. She's a fashionista, so she's done the homework and knows what I need. Thank God." She looked at Nia, and saw a tense look cover her face. "It's not that bad, Nia. Lighten up. I mean, what else do you have to do? Really?" She stopped in front of a sunglasses cart, then picked up a pair and tried them on. She turned to Nia. "What do you think? Kinda hot, huh?" she asked, then turned and looked at herself in the mirror. The glasses were knockoffs, but nice.

Nia shook her head. "You're asking the wrong person. I keep telling you that my sister is the shopper."

Charly pushed a pair on Nia's face, then reached up and adjusted the arms over her ears. "Cute! And you only said that once, by the way. And I'm not here with your sister. I'm with you. And these are fab on you." The sunglasses did look good on Nia, and Nia would have them, she decided. Charly knew Nia came from money— or at least her father had some—but she didn't care about labels or putting on airs. Three bucks or three thousand didn't matter to her as long as she liked something. Nia took off the shades, then tried to set them back on the cart. Charly pushed her hand away before she could. "C'mon, Nia. Have fun for a change. You know there's nothing wrong with cute," she said, digging in her bag to retrieve her wallet.

The sunglass man waved his hand, refusing to take payment. He pointed to the cameras and the vending cart's sign, then smiled. "Are you kidding me? You just

gave me free publicity. No way I'm taking your money.
Why are you here, anyway? I can tell you girls are fa-
mous."

Charly smiled, then elbowed Nia. "See, even he knows
there's a hot girl hiding somewhere behind all of this
don't-look-at-me façade," she teased, and to her surprise
Nia almost smiled, then slipped the shades back on. It
wasn't a bonafide grin, but she could tell it made Nia feel
good, just as Trent had.

"So, what's up with you and this Trent guy?" she
asked, walking away from the sunglasses stand.

Nia shrugged, keeping pace with her. "I don't know
what you mean." She opened her purse, then took out
the car keys.

Charly stopped in the middle of the mall, flipped her
hair, then rolled her eyes. She couldn't believe Nia's
nerve. "Are you kidding me? Do you think I'm blind or
numb or just plain dumb? I just wanna know what kind
of fool you take me for." Her words came out flippant,
but she couldn't help it. She didn't like anyone playing on
her intelligence.

Nia's whole face seemed to stretch in shock, and
Charly could tell she wasn't used to someone being so
blatant. "What do you mean? And why are you talking
to me like that?" Her question was just that, an inquiry
that held no ounce of guts.

Charly's hand was on her hip while she tried to turn
down her attitude that was beginning to rise. She couldn't
just be flippant with Nia, could she? After all, the girl was
her project, not her friend or someone off the streets, so
she couldn't just handle her. But that's what she was there

for, she reminded herself. She was supposed to bring Nia to life, and no one said she couldn't give her a backbone. If life was just fight or flight, Nia had most definitely chosen flight. She'd given in and caved to whatever, while her sister did the opposite. Charly shook her head. She wasn't having that. "Nia, if we're gonna be friends, we're gonna have to respect each other. That means don't play me."

Nia shook her head. "We're not friends, Charly. You're here to help my dad. After that, you'll be gone." Her words were final and held no feeling.

Charly's attitude dwindled. Nia was right, and she had to respect that. The girl did have good sense, she'd give her that. But she wouldn't give her a pass on everything. Her finishing what she'd come to do didn't allow for passes or excuses. "You're right; we're not friends, and after this, I may never come here again. But that doesn't change the fact that you're trying to play me. If you don't want to admit that you're interested in Trent, that's cool. It's not my business. But, and I stress *but,* let's be clear. Anyone with vision can see you think Trent's hot, and would've been able to feel your attraction to him—including him," she began, then felt her pocket vibrating. "One sec." She removed her phone, and saw Liam's name register on the screen. "I was just going to help you snag him, that's all," she said, then turned her attention away from Nia and answered Liam's call. She walked as she talked.

"Hey, love, are you free?" his delicious voice asked. His English accent seemed thicker, and drew her in with each syllable.

She felt herself blush, and she gulped. *Why am I suddenly feeling you?* Charly wanted to ask him, but instead said, "No. Why? What's up? Do you need me?"

Liam's flirtatious laugh met her ears from the other end. "Well, love, since you asked. Yes, I do need you. Wait. Hold on a second, love. Don't hang up," he said, then started talking to someone in the background, and not just any someone, Charly discovered when she heard a voice cooing. It was all soft and feminine and out of order. Whoever it was was pushing, asking him out.

"Liam! Liam!" she called out, trying to get him to hear her over whomever. "Liam?"

"I really can't," he said, still talking to the girl in the background, his "can't" sounding like "cahnt." "No. no. I'm single, but it's against studio policy," he continued to explain.

Charly was getting more incensed with each word and pause. What did he mean he was single? Since the last *Extreme Dream Team* season, the world thought they were together, and that should've meant something, as far as she was concerned. "Who are you talking to, Liam? Why are you explaining yourself?" she asked, then looked at her screen. Surely, they were disconnected. They had to be since he wasn't answering her. She shook her head, seeing the seconds on the digital timer increase, which meant they were still connected. "Whatever," she said, then ended the call.

A slight laugh pulled her attention, making her turn around.

"So, what's up with you and this Liam guy?" Nia asked, shooting Charly a knowing look. "If you don't want to admit that you're in to Liam, it's cool. It's not my business. But it's obvious," she said, throwing Charly's words back at her. "So don't try to play me." A so-there smile spread across her face.

Nia had called her out, and she had no rebuttal. She could see dealing with a smart girl was going to be a test of will and truths, and her sharpness wasn't reserved for her nerdiness or book intelligence. Nia also had a mouth, one that wasn't always afraid of speaking out, which should've been a good thing, but not this time. Charly rolled her eyes. There was no way she could really defend herself, so she decided to throw Nia some hush words, too. "And don't you play me, either. We're not friends. Remember? Those are your words." She twisted her face, catching herself. Being checked by Nia or not, she couldn't sway from the game plan, not if she wanted to succeed with the mission. She plastered on a phony smile. "Let's just call it a wrap. Nothing here is moving my imagination for ideas for your dad's office. Let's just go back to the pharmacy again, so I can get my prescription and get out of your way. Me and Liam got a lot of work to do, and I wanna get it right for your father. Deal?"

6

There was a problem. A pressing issue that had nothing to do with making over Nia or her domain had changed the game when Charly walked into the hotel. As soon as she checked in and retrieved her room key, she spotted Liam sitting in one of the lounge chairs in the lobby. His face bore a confused look of glee and uncertainty. One hand was on the arm of the high-back chair, the other rested on top of a large suitcase. Charly raised her brows in question, then she flared her nostrils. He'd been demoted from her list of favorite people since their conversation hours ago, and she didn't really feel like having a long drawn-out discussion with him about why she'd refused all of his calls after she'd hung up on him. She just wasn't up for it. Her feet hurt, her back ached, and her temples were lightly throbbing. Her day with Nia had finally come to a close, and she couldn't have been happier.

Nia had been a task, refusing to give in. She'd turned down everything but the sunglasses, which she seemed to covet, and that was probably because she could hide behind them. After that, Charly had tried just about everything she could to get Nia to see things her way. But other than scouting for design ideas for her dad's office, she wasn't up for trying anything new. Clothes. Purses. Makeup. *Nothing,* Charly thought. She'd thrown Nia every bone she thought a teen girl would chase, and Nia had slapped them away, one by one, insisting she was happy the way she was.

Liam waved and pressed his lips together as Charly walked off the marble floor and onto the carpeted area. She padded toward him. "How goes it, love?" he asked.

"*Now* it goes better, I hope," she said, releasing her weight into a chair across from his. She put up her feet on the circular table that separated them, and released her frustration in a loud exhale. "Everything I have hurts, and I can't wait to take it in," she said, referring to going to bed.

Liam flipped over his wrist and looked at the face of his watch. He shook his head in the negative. "Too early, love." He sat taller, then looked around. "Where's the camera crew? I've been waiting for them."

Charly shrugged. "Who knows? I lost them back at the mall. They said they got all the footage they needed, then they bounced."

"What?" he asked, startled. "They can't do that."

Charly rubbed her temples. "Why not, Liam?"

"Because."

Charly looked at him. He was so much smarter than answering a question with because. "That's not an answer, and you know it. Because what? Why can't they?"

He exhaled. "Because you're supposed to have a guardian. They're the only adults here. They can't just leave us alone," he answered in clipped, frustrated sentences.

Charly laughed. "Calm down, pretty boy. I said they bounced, not that they up and left the country. I'm sure they just went to grab a bite or something. Besides, when did we ever have twenty-four/seven coverage? Everyone gets time off. We need to eat, sleep, go to the bathroom," she said, gesturing with her hands as she spoke. "What are you afraid of? Being alone? Sounds to me like *you* need a guardian. Don't put that on me. I've been watching myself since I was seven," she said, then thought of how her mother used to leave her alone. She shook her head.

Liam reared back his head. "Afraid of being alone? Me, Mr. Travel the Globe *Alone?* I'm not scared of anything, love. You can't be serious!"

Charly nodded, enjoying getting him riled up. He'd caused her blood pressure to rise with his "I'm single" earlier, and she was happy to return the unwanted favor. "We all have weaknesses and idiosyncrasies."

"Well, if that's the case, my weakness is figuring out where to sleep tonight. Some pipe burst or something, and they've shut down every floor but this one and the second one, so there's no room for me." He patted his suitcase. "And someone's losing their job behind this one. I can guarantee you that."

Charly drew her brows together. "Either I'm tired or I'm just slow. Explain again."

Liam sat up. "They messed up on the rooms. The studio. Your room and the camera crew's room are booked here, but who knows where I'm booked? The hotel and I called the other local hotels, and no one has a reservation for me. No one. And I called the studio and Mr. Day, and wouldn't you friggin' know it—he's in the sky somewhere, so, of course, his phone is powered down."

Charly's eyes almost crossed, and not because she was tired. She couldn't believe Liam was making such a big deal out of not having a place to sleep. It was still pretty early, so there was plenty of time for him to arrange accommodations. "Don't worry about it," she said, getting up. "Us sitting here talking about it isn't going to fix it." She got up and stood in front of him, her hand on her hip. "C'mon. Let's go to my room."

Liam's head shook adamantly. "No, love. No way. I'm not going to impose on you. Girls need space and, besides, it won't look good for us to be bunked together."

Charly's eyes bore into his and she frowned. "Please, Liam. Stop it. It's not an invitation to sleep over, it's an invitation to get you out of this lobby." She shrugged. "But if you wanna stay here and wait on the camera crew, be my guest. I'm out," she said, then walked away, beelining to the elevator and jumping on. She pressed the second floor button, then mashed another to close the doors. She needed them to shut quickly. Charly wanted to make it to her room and lock herself in before he could change his mind about the offer. She didn't want Liam to be stuck in the lobby looking like a squatter, but, on the other hand, she didn't want him in her space either. It would end up being uncomfortable, she convinced herself. Their being so close without adult supervision or distraction wasn't smart, not after the way he'd been affecting her feelings lately.

The elevator shot up for a second, then halted smoothly. The doors parted. Charly stepped off and read the sign that displayed the room numbers, then followed the arrow to the left where hers was located. Rotating her neck, she tried to work out the kinks, and begged her feet to stop hurting. "I can't wait to get out of these shoes," she said aloud, louder than she planned.

"Well, you should let me help you," Liam's voice said from behind, making her jump.

"What the . . . ?" Charly said, turning. "How did you . . . ?"

Liam was walking toward her, rolling suitcases behind him. He made a face. "The stairs, love. I told you only the lobby and the second floor aren't shut down." He looked down at his legs. "With all the working out and running I do, a flight of steps is easy. I brought your bags," he informed, catching up to her. "You forgot to get them, and since I was coming up anyway, I didn't see the need of making the staff work."

Charly crinkled her eyebrows together, then turned. Her room was only a few doors down, and she couldn't wait to get there. She didn't know how the chemistry thing between her and Liam would work out, but she could handle it. All she had to do was keep her emotions in check, she told herself. It wasn't as if she'd shared her feelings with him. Really, she wasn't even sure if they existed at all or if he just seemed more appealing, and alluring didn't necessary equate to real attraction. *Right?* she questioned herself, making it to the hotel room door, and sliding the card key in the slot until she heard the lock release.

Liam was behind her, reaching around and turning the door handle before she knew it. He pushed it open so Charly could enter. "Hurry up, love. I'll wait my turn." He walked in, rolling the stacked luggage behind him, then made his way to the desk area in the corner of the midsized room.

"What?" Charly asked. "Hurry up and do what?" She followed in his footsteps, but stopped at the bed. She climbed on the mattress, then crawled her way toward the headboard, then released her weight onto the plush pillows. "Ahh," she moaned, enjoying the cushioning. "Please don't say anything stupid, Liam. I just wanna lie right here. I'm *so* tired." She stared at the ceiling, then shut her eyes, more exhausted than she'd realized.

"Me, too," Liam said, his voice growing closer.

Charly felt the bed sink under Liam's weight as he climbed onto the mattress, but she didn't care. He could lie there for as long as he wanted, as long as he didn't interrupt her sleep. She felt an almost comatose state pulling her into slumber, and her head was getting heavier, becoming one with the pillow. It took all of her might to open her lids and glance at him beside her. Liam was on his side with his body turned in the opposite direction of hers. She watched as his shoulder rose and fell in millimeters, in tune with his breathing. She rolled over, facing away from him, then let her eyes rest. All she needed was an hour, she told her internal clock. In sixty minutes, she'd be up and ready for the world. "Three thousand and six hundred seconds . . ." she whispered.

Charly's eyes shot open, and she froze. She was surrounded by pitch blackness, and someone was shaking her. Her heart raced and adrenaline pushed heat through her veins. There was no way this was happening. She'd heard of lucid dreams, but this was ridiculous. She knew she could control herself if it were indeed a lucid dream, but could she also feel in one? "Stop it!" she said, covering her ears and kicking with all her might.

"Ouch!" the owner of the hand tapping her hip said in a much-too-familiar voice.

She sat up. "Liam?"

He started laughing. "Talk about a rough sleeper!"

Charly looked around, trying to make him out in the dark. Then she panicked. How long had they been asleep?

"Get up, love. It's almost daylight," he said, answering her unspoken question. The lamp turned on, blinding her. Liam moved the clock on the nightstand to where he could see it, then groaned. He turned toward her and propped himself up on his elbow, then looked in her eyes. His expression was uncertain. "Well, I guess we spent the night together . . ." he said, his exclamation cutting through them both.

Charly's head dropped. They had spent the night together, but all they'd done was sleep, and she didn't even remember doing that. But if the studio heads found out— if anyone returned his calls and knew that Liam didn't have a room, and if the camera crew didn't see him in the lobby—that could be the end of the show, and they both knew it.

"It'll be okay, love. No one knows, and no one has to," he said, getting off the bed. "I'm going to hop in the shower and get dressed. You can finish sleeping. I got some things to take care of, then I'll swing by and get you." He opened one of his suitcases, grabbed some of his things, then headed toward the bathroom. "Oh, no." His voice held a trace of woe. "Charly, love? There's a problem." He made his way back to her, then held out a bright wrapper to her. "I guess someone slipped this under the door while we were sleeping."

Charly yawned and stretched. "Liam, make sure you come swoop me as soon as you finish. I got a lot to do, starting with Nia," she said, then took the wrapper from him, noticing it was ripped in half. Her eyes stretched in curiosity and panic. Someone knew she and Liam had spent the night together, and there was no denying it. The empty Skittles package with black marker written on both sides of it told her so, and she and Liam weren't the only thing it addressed.

Charly, you're being played. Everything isn't what it seems. Hi, Liam, hope you two enjoyed your night together.

7

Charly drummed on the counter, then rang the bell. She'd been at the hotel reception desk for what seemed like forever, and saw no movement. She looked around, then made a full pivot in search of someone she could flag down. Surely, there had to be someone working. Though the town was small, the lodging was upscale, which should've equated to top-tier hospitality. But how could they provide that if no one was there to help her? she thought. With her body turned sideways, she reached back over and pounded the little button on the dome until the bell sang.

"How can I help you?" a dry familiar voice said. "I'm sorry if you were waiting. Have you been here long?"

She jumped a little because she didn't hear anyone approach. Charly turned, covering her heart to slow the racing, ready to turn on false charm, but then stopped. Heaven's emotionless face greeted her. Her makeup still looked like she was from an eighties rock and roll group, and her hair said her surname should've been Marley. Her gap-toothed sneer was cold. "Oh, hi, Heaven. I was just getting ready to walk around there to see what could've possibly been taking someone forever, which is exactly how long I've been here." She swooped her hair from out of her eye. "Question?" she said.

"Answer," Heaven replied, her face still stone. She mimicked Charly, and pretended to push hair out of her eyes.

Charly didn't care what Liam said the day before, she wasn't going to bite her tongue or keep herself in check. This Heaven girl clearly had something stuck up her rear end and was taking it out on the world, which would've been fine if Charly were from somewhere else, but she wasn't. She was down on earth and was more than ready to snatch Heaven back down to it. She shook her head and smirked. "Listen, Heaven, it's clear you don't like your job, but that's not my fault. And that's cool, you don't have to, but what you do have to do—what you're gonna do—is respect me," she said, waving her finger in the air. "Or . . ." She stopped herself from threatening her, imagining how the headlines would read. DIVA CHARLY FROM THE *extreme dream team* BEATS DOWN INNOCENT HOTEL WORKER. "Or, I'll make sure you lose your job," she said, then leaned on the counter and stared at an unmoved Heaven.

Another hotel employee walked behind the counter, giving Charly a pleasant nod. From his polished appearance and fine suit, Charly could tell he was the manager.

"What's your question?" Heaven asked, her tone barely different, despite her boss being present.

Charly squared her shoulders, then asked Heaven if she'd seen anyone or anything strange, inquired if any of the other hotel workers had, then relayed the story of something being slipped under her door. Heaven shook her head, then burst out laughing in Charly's face. "I've been here all night, and what do you think I've seen? Look around, and you tell me. Look at the people. Do *you* see anyone strange? There is a Sci-Fi conference going on."

The small downtown area was crowded. Sci-Fi conference goers, she reminded herself, making her way onto the walk and looking toward the street for a taxi. She'd called Liam five times in two minutes and kept being sent straight to voice mail. She was growing irritated. It was still breakfast time, and already people were bumping into her, and not getting through to Liam wasn't good, not to mention being haunted by a candy company's product. The Skittles wrapper was burned into her memory and haunting her. She was still peeved from Heaven having the gall to laugh in her face. She looked around at the people costumed like they'd been featured in science fiction movies and television shows, and her irritation melted. She knew why Heaven had been so tickled. Just about everyone around them could've been classified as questionable if their outfits were taken into consideration. Still, feeling less aggravated or not, she wasn't comfortable. If whoever had slipped the candy wrapper under her room door knew that Liam stayed all night in her room, she was certain the studio could find out too, which would more than likely mean the demise of she and Liam being on the same show. But that was only the tip of her worry. Now she didn't feel safe in the hotel, and had to find a reason to be relocated. She couldn't just tell Mr. Day what happened because he might investigate, and then she and Liam's innocent night would be discovered and, probably, blown out of proportion.

"Over here, Charly," one of the hotel employees called, waving his arm in the air to get her attention. "Can I help you with something? You look lost," he said from by the curb.

Charly looked past two people dressed as aliens and waved back, then made her way to the hotel employee, hoping he could flag her a cab. She smiled, but still couldn't shake the thought of the candy wrapper and the message. Who was playing her? she wondered, walking and not paying attention. She had to get to Nia today, but she needed to hunt down Rory first. Rory was her key to everything, or so she'd said. Charly hoped Rory was right, and wasn't just fighting for the attention of whom she considered to be a television star, instead of just being there to help her friend.

"Whoa," the guy said, his arm crossing her waist and pushing back. She was so lost in thoughts she'd almost stepped into the street. "I apologize, miss, but you almost stepped in the street."

"Thank you," Charly said, looking side to side. "I need a cab," she said.

"Oh." He pressed his lips together in thought, then ran his hand through his hair. His eyebrows crinkled and so did his nose. "Well . . . miss, we don't get that much traffic around here. We're not that busy and, honestly, we don't have a car service in *town* anymore. We don't normally have many visitors—this is even our first Sci-Fi conference, and that's 'cause of some book that used our name." He nodded, clearly impressed. "But I can call a car for you, but he's coming from the town next door, so it'll take him a little bit to get here."

Charly looked at her watch. She did need to get to Nia, but she had some time. "Okay. Please do that for me," she said, then crossed her arms, waiting.

In seconds, he'd whipped out his phone and was talking to someone named Jake. His expression twisted again as he moved the phone to his side. "Sorry, Jake said he can't come today. The alternator died on his car, and Revy—the mechanic—she can't fix it until tomorrow. Jake said he can be here before noon though." He extended the phone to Charly. "Wanna speak to him?"

It took everything Charly had not to roll her eyes. "No, thank you. Tell Jake I hope his car gets fixed soon," she said, walking away, thinking the hotel worker had to be wrong. The street was filled with people; surely someone had to be providing car service. Besides that, there had to be public transportation, she thought, making her way to the corner in search of a bus stop sign. None was there, so she about-faced, speed walking toward the hotel.

"Anything else, miss?" the hotel worker asked, as Charly made her way back over to him.

She paused before she spoke, reminding herself it wasn't his fault that his town was on pause. "You guys do have a bus around here, right? I mean everyone has a bus, some form of public transportation."

He nodded. "Of course, if you tell me where you're going, I can tell you how to get there."

Relief coursed through Charly's veins. She whipped out her phone, found Rory's address, then handed it to him.

This time his face twisted like it was in a vise. "I can tell you how to catch the bus just about everywhere else but there. You can only get there by car. I'm sorry." He gave back her phone.

Charly raked her fingers through her hair. This was going to be harder than she thought. "It's not your fault," she reminded him and herself. She scrolled through her numbers, found one of the cameramen's numbers, then dialed. "No! Not straight to voice mail. I need to switch phone carriers," she whined. "Is there no reception in this town?"

"Uh-um. Uh-um." The hotel guy was clearing his throat. "I think I have a plan for how you can get a ride to where you want to go," he said, pointing behind Charly. "My girl over there. She just got off and lives out that way. Maybe she'll take you."

Charly turned around. "Oh, gawd," she said. The guy was pointing to Heaven.

8

She was not swallowing her pride or eating her words. Those were two things that crossed Charly's mind as she called out to stop Heaven in her tracks. When the morbid-looking girl paused midstride, then turned and locked eyes with Charly, the other thing that plagued her was there was no way she was going to kiss this girl's butt for a ride either. If it were up to her, she wouldn't be talking to her at all. Her phone vibrated in her hand, and she relaxed a little, hoping it was Liam or the camera crew returning one of her calls. She looked at her cell, and knew God was paying her back for something. It was only an e-mail alert.

"What is it? I'm off," Heaven said, crossing her arms and looking about as excited as a pallbearer.

Charly silently counted backward from ten to calm herself before she snapped. Since she wanted a ride, the last thing she could do was tell Heaven where she could

go and how fast to get there, and the destination was opposite of the girl's name. "Aren't you supposed to have
like an extra shot of energy or something?" Charly asked,
trying to make light of the situation. "I thought everyone
felt that way when they got off work. At least I do."

Heaven just raised her brows.

"So . . ." she began, not knowing what to say. She and
Heaven kept bumping heads, and asking her for a ride
was the last thing Charly wanted to do. She didn't want
to give Heaven the opportunity to reject her, especially
when she needed her. She decided that honesty was the
best policy. Truth and the almighty dollar would hopefully work. "Listen, Heaven, I know I'm not your favorite, and that's fine. But I really need you—the show
needs you. And I'm willing to pay."

Heaven's eyebrows rose. "Need *me*? For what?" Her
arms were still crossed, but her tone held interest.

Charly gulped. Pride was hard to swallow. "I need a
ride." Heaven started to shake her head no. "It's not out
of your way, according to him," Charly said, pointing
back toward the hotel worker who'd directed her to
Heaven.

Heaven lifted herself on tiptoe, following Charly's finger toward the guy. She resumed her position, then adjusted her attitude a bit. "Oh, Mike sent you to me.
That's different . . . it changes things. What's up? Where
do you need to go?" Heaven asked.

Charly didn't know what made it so different, and she
dared not ask. All she cared about was getting to Rory as
quickly as possible so she could get to Nia. She scrolled
through her contacts until she reached Rory's name.

"Here. I need to go to this address," she said, handing Heaven the phone.

Heaven's eyes stretched. "Really? You want to go to this address? You sure?" She drew her brows together and nodded with each question, then closed her eyes and shook her head during the brief pauses in between, then began the nod and shake again, as if she were answering each inquiry the way she wanted Charly to.

Charly almost asked Heaven why it was such a big deal and why she kept nodding and shaking her head like Charly needed her to answer for her, but thought better of it. The less Heaven knew, the better, she thought. She did have to admit though, the line of questioning piqued her interest. What was the big deal about going to Rory's? She nodded. Whatever it was about the address just was. She didn't have time to explain why she needed to go, she just did. "Yes, I'm sure."

Heaven pressed her lips together, then looked over to where Mike was standing. She shrugged. "Okay, come on, but don't complain about my ride. It gets me where I need to go." Her words were still as dry as she was dreary. She reached down, took a set of keys off a pocket chain, then walked.

Charly followed behind her, trying to keep up and swallowing her distaste for the pocket chain. She shook her head, wondering who still wore those, then remembered Heaven was a little different. Everyone she'd met in the town was unusual compared to what she was used to. "Are we almost there?" she asked Heaven, who was speed walking. They'd rounded the corner, walked a block, and didn't seem like they were stopping soon.

Heaven only nodded, then crossed the street. She zoomed into a gravel parking lot that had seen better days. Holes and debris were everywhere, along with a couple of homeless people whom Charly was surprised to see. It wasn't that she wasn't used to seeing them. New York and Chicago were filled with them, but she didn't expect a small town to have outside residents. Heaven waved her hand in the air, then made her way to the back of the odd-shaped space, stopping in front of a stack of boxes. She looked around like someone was after her.

"You're good, Heaven. I've been watching out," a voice said from somewhere Charly couldn't pinpoint.

"Thanks, Oracle," Heaven said. "You always do, but since I didn't see you, I wasn't sure if you had gone to save the world." Heaven looked toward a broken-down van that looked like it had been borrowed from a Scooby-Doo movie.

The back door slid open, and a woman stuck out her head. Like Heaven, she had dreadlocks, but hers were wrapped in fabric to the top of her head, then cascaded down like a weeping willow. Her gray hair framed a soft face that looked like it'd been formed out of red Georgia clay, and shiny lips spread into a smile when she looked at Charly. "Oh, company? That's unusual," she said, then locked eyes with Charly. "They call me Oracle," she introduced herself. "I'm from the Sky family."

"Oracle? That's nice," Charly said, not knowing how to respond, and almost afraid to. If the woman was called the Oracle that meant she was insightful, well, at least according to the old *Matrix* movie she'd watched over and over. Dr. Deveraux El, an older gentleman from back home in Illinois, who'd been schooling her on history and culture had urged her to watch it, encouraged her to wake up. He'd said life was not what everyone was programmed to believe—it was much more. Charly nodded. That was the same thing the woman called the Oracle in the movie had said too.

Heaven looked at Charly, then Oracle. She shrugged, then began moving bricks and boxes.

"Yes, my name is Oracle, and thank you. And you're Charly." She informed Charly of her own name as if Charly didn't know her parents had named her Charly, then Oracle turned to Heaven. "This one is here to save the world." Oracle pointed to Charly. "So I get a day off." She laughed, then winked at Charly. "I know who you are."

"Okay," Charly said, then began helping Heaven move the last remaining boxes, revealing an older motorcycle that Charly assumed had to be Heaven's ride.

"Let's go," Heaven said, unlocking a helmet, then strapping her bag on the back of the motorcycle. She straddled the seat, then waited for Charly to mount it. "Here," she said, handing Charly the headgear. "Hopefully, we'll get where we're going without getting pulled over. I only have one, but I don't like to wear them anyway. My hair doesn't fit." She turned on the ignition, revved the engine with a twist of her wrist, then took off. She pit stopped next to the old van, dug in her pocket, then pulled out a sandwich bag and handed it to Oracle. "Your herbs. Echinacea, organic rose petals, and lavender."

Charly thought she was going to die. D. I. E. She was on the back of Heaven's raggedy motorcycle, holding on for her life. She closed her eyes and pressed her helmeted head against Heaven's back, feeling her body angle right, then left, as they zoomed at top speed, rounding curves. The engine roared, deafening her, then it backfired, sounding like gunshots blasting. She almost swallowed her tongue, she was so afraid. They rounded a corner and drove down a winding street for what seemed like forever before Heaven finally took a sharp turn onto a dirt path, then shifted into a lower gear until they began gliding. The motorcycle slowed to a stop.

"That's it over there," Heaven said, pointing to a house out in the distance. "This is as far as I go."

Charly got off, then unstrapped the helmet from her chin. "Okay," she said, then looked in the direction Heaven was pointing. "Serious? You can't take me a little farther?" She slipped her purse off her shoulder and dug inside. "I told you I'm paying."

Heaven laughed. "It's not the money I'm concerned about, it's the cost," she said, working her head into the helmet. "You'll see" were her last words before she revved the engine, turned the bike around, and sped off.

Charly watched Heaven disappear down the drive, then looked down to her shoes. Her heels were almost four inches high, and her toes were exposed. Her eyes traveled to the dirt road that served as a driveway, then took in all the rocks that were scattered along the way. She shook her head and tried to swallow the pain that she was certain was going to set in. She hadn't even walked one step, and already her feet were hurting.

9

A scream cut through the air, followed by a barrage of curse words. Charly paused, and tried to keep her uncomfortable stance. She'd walked the long drive with her weight on the front of her feet because her heels kept getting stuck in the dirt. A crash made her eyebrows rise, and she wondered what was going on. She gripped her bag to her side, then looked on the ground for something she could use to protect herself if she had to. She'd come too far to turn around, but she wasn't certain about moving forward. But what else could she do? She was in the middle of nowhere, and had no other way to leave except by foot, and hers were hurting too much to accomplish that without her soles catching fire. A crash similar to dishes hitting a wall sounded through the opened windows of the eyesore of a dilapidated house. It was two stories high, painted an awful lemon yellow, and had baby blue shutters. Suddenly, all was quiet. Charly stood in place waiting to see if it was safe to approach. She reached into her purse and retrieved her cell phone. She shook her head. It still had no reception. She exhaled, put it back, then walked on tiptoe toward the now-quiet house.

She'd just passed a broken-down car that was supported by bricks instead of tires, and was almost to the porch when a larger girl burst through the screen door at top speed, then leaped off the porch. Her hair was wrapped around her head, held in place by gobs of silver duckbill clips, and shoes were in her hands. She paced back and forth, swinging the low heels back and forth like weapons. "Bring it! Come on out here, so we can do this. It was an accident, and you know it. Now you wanna act stupid after I just got my feet and hands did?" She threw up her hands, pointing the tips of the shoes toward the sun. She was still moving. "Really? You just want to mess up me getting my pretty swag on. I got things to do, so hurry up and come get this beat down," she invited, stopping and facing the front door. " 'Come on, bring it. My nails are messed up now, so ain't no sense in wasting it. Bring it. I got something for you."

Charly took it all in, and hoped the angry girl in front of her wasn't Rory, but, deep down, she knew it was. Who else talked about getting their pretty on? "Rory?" she said, much lower than she'd expected to.

"Yayer!" The girl moved back and forth like a bull getting ready to charge, then started hiking up her fitted hot pink sweats. "Come on. I'm waiting. I been wanting to connect my foot to your butt all week."

"Rory?" Charly called out a little louder.

The girl turned and looked at Charly. Fire was in her eyes and her nostrils flared as her chest rose and dropped with every breath. Every heave could be heard, making Charly question if she had asthma. When the girl took a step forward, looking like she was ready to pounce, Charly wondered if she'd have to fight. The rage in the air was thick enough for Charly to feel it, and, for seconds, time froze. Everything disappeared as Charly's survival instinct kicked in. Charly no longer cared that she was in the middle of God knew where or how mad the girl thought she was, Charly was ready and skilled. She'd learned how to hook with the best of them back in Illinois, and would've been more than willing to introduce the girl to two fists and a head split if needed.

"Charly?" the girl asked, and time ticked again. "What you doing here?" she asked, switching personalities and cutting off her anger. "Charly, my girl. Whazzup?" She smiled, making her way over to where Charly stood.

"Rory? I thought that was you—" Charly began, then pointed. A large woman was making her way down the porch steps at top speed. In one hand there was a cast-iron frying pan, and in the other was a bat. "Rory, look out."

Rory turned around and looked over her shoulder. "Oh, no," she said, then picked up speed, moving toward Charly, then grabbing her hand. "I hope you can run, Charly. She's big, but she can move!" Rory yelled as the two of them made tracks through the grass, then over the dirt path that served as the driveway.

Charly felt like she was in the middle of a low-budget film, pushing her way through tall trees and bushes, unable to feel the branches scrape her skin or the rocky terrain pressing against the bottoms of her feet. A shotgun cut loudly through the air, and her heart caught in her throat. "Where did that come from? I thought she had a bat! What did you do?" she asked Rory, who was still pulling her.

Rory rounded a wooden shack, then stopped. Her eyes moved left and right as she took in their surroundings. "That wasn't no bat, that's her shotgun. Now hurry up. Sit down," she instructed Charly, then crouched. She shielded her eyes from the sun to survey the bushes, then finally sat. She stretched her legs in front of her, then held her hand to her chest until her breathing softened. "We have about five minutes before she realizes which hiding spot I'm in."

Charly tilted her head. She couldn't have heard right, she told herself. Not now, not when her feet felt like someone had shot nails through them. "Serious? Rory, what did you do?"

Rory threw back her head and laughed from deep down in her belly. She grabbed her midsection, and tried to pull down her white tank top over her exposed stomach, but there was just too much stomach to do so. "Sis, last night I accidentally dropped Skittles in the sink, and today I ate the last piece of cake. That's it and that's all." She shook her head.

"*What?*" Charly began, then was interrupted by the sound of a shotgun cutting through the air. She was on her feet before she knew it, running to wherever. She wanted no part of Rory and her sweet tooth or the problems that came with them, but felt like she needed to hide.

"This way," Rory said, running around the shack, and

heading toward a car. She dug in her bra while her feet were in motion, pulled out a key, then cried out in pain.

Charly watched as Rory's almost two-hundred-plus pounds flew through the air as if she had sprouted wings, then closed her eyes when she saw Rory headed toward the ground. A th-thump noise let her know that Rory had landed and, more than likely, had bounced. Charly opened her lids, then held her breath. Rory was spread out on the ground, facedown with her legs splayed. She moaned. Charly ran over to her. "You all right?"

Rory tried to shake her head, but stopped midway. "I think I broke my toe and my head," she began, then stopped when another shot was heard. "Man, we gotta go, Charly, or my auntie will shoot both of us."

Charly laughed. She couldn't help it. The whole display had been more than she could stand, and she was sure someone somewhere was filming her. What was going down just couldn't be for real. "No, she wouldn't," Charly said. "That's your family."

Rory held out her arm, then turned her wrist. There was a small circular scar on the inside of her bicep. "Yes, she would. Again."

Another gunshot cut through the summer day, and was louder than before, a sign of Rory's aunt being closer to them. Charly reached down and pulled up Rory, then helped her hop to the car on her one good foot.

"You're gonna have to drive, Charly. I can't."

Charly gulped. The last time she drove, she'd pulled directly into a ditch. "I don't know . . ." One more shot rounded off. "Okay. Give me the keys. Give me the keys!" Charly said twice, then helped Rory into the passenger seat. She'd closed the door and was around the car in the driver seat before she knew it. She stuck the key in the ignition, but it wouldn't turn.

Rory shook her head, then pressed the key farther into the ignition until they heard a slight click. "Here. Hold this in place. It doesn't fully work, meaning it won't turn. I really don't think it ever has. But if you keep it pressed in . . ." She reached over, fiddled with some wiring under the steering wheel, and the car came to life. "Tah-dah, it'll make it start." She shook her head. "Ghetto, I know, but nobody has money around here to get locks and ignitions changed. We just rewire it," she said, looking around.

Uncertainty was tugging at Charly. The car wasn't parked at Rory's, so maybe it wasn't hers, but she did have a key. "Are you sure it's okay for me to drive? You were stuck before, so that means it can't be yours."

Rory shook her head, looking around. "It's cool, Charly. I don't always have access to it. Besides, everyone else has driven it, so why not you? I drive it, Nia has, Mya has. You name 'em, they've whipped it." Her eyes widened. "Now go. Go! She's coming. Hurry and hang a left."

Charly threw the car in DRIVE, then sped off, leaving a trail of dirt floating in the air as she made her way to the end of the driveway. She strapped on her seat belt, then turned onto the street. With her foot pressed on the accelerator, she tried to figure out what had just happened. How had everything gone from bad to worse in a matter of seconds? Sure, she'd gone through some tough times, but she'd never had someone shooting at her. She was just about to speak when she felt her purse vibrating against her side. She exhaled, glad that she finally had phone reception. It had to be Liam or the camera crew, she believed, reaching into her bag and grabbing the cell to answer it. Liam's name floated across the screen, and Charly's adrenaline slowed. Finally, a break, she told herself, then accepted his call. "Hello?" she began, then noticed the blue lights flashing behind her. She dropped the phone in her lap. She hoped the cops didn't see her talking on the cell while driving. "Don't hang up, Liam! Five-oh's behind me!" she yelled.

"It's the Po Po, Charly girl. You better pull over, 'cause I don't feel like going back to jail," Rory demanded, slapping her palm against the dashboard.

10

"Ridiculous. Freaking ridiculous," Charly muttered in disbelief. Of all things that could've possibly happened while trying to complete the Save Nia mission, she never would have guessed that jail would've been one. She looked out the backseat window at Rory, who just stood there looking stupid and shrugging, and instantly wanted to kill her. Being locked up may have not moved Rory because, obviously, she'd been behind bars before, but for Charly it spelled doom and demise. She wasn't a criminal, had never been, but now she was sitting in the back of a police car like one, while Rory waved from the side of the road. If Charly could've flipped her the bird, she would've, but even that wasn't possible. With her hands cuffed behind her back and being locked inside, a lot of things were beyond her reach, namely, getting to Nia.

"I'mma come get you, sis. You're good, Charly girl,"

Rory was yelling at the back window as the police cruiser pulled off.

Charly shook her head. How was Rory going to help her when she wasn't even powerful enough to help herself? She couldn't even get out of East Jesus, as she'd referred to her town.

The cop looked at her in his rearview mirror and nodded a little. "I wouldn't have cuffed you if it were up to me, but we don't know you around here. You could be anybody."

Charly just shot daggers at him. They'd gone over whom she was, why she was there, and even Rory had admitted that she'd asked Charly to drive, but Officer Unfriendly didn't care for several reasons. Charly didn't have a license. The owner of the car, whom they'd called, met them roadside and said he didn't know her. His declaration was the determining factor. It didn't matter that Rory had never received permission to drive the car or that it was her idea to steal it or that she hadn't informed Charly of the theft, but instead, made it seem as if it were fine with them to drive. The only thing that counted was that Charly was behind the wheel. She'd tried her best to convince them about the real truth, but no one took her seriously. When she'd mentioned that she was a reality television star who was there to help the mayor, they'd laughed in her face, then questioned how a teenage girl—especially one who was hanging with Rory—could possibly help the mayor.

The officer spread his lips, then shook his head at her while he smiled. "You know you can do so much more with your life . . . Charly, right? You have school, college if you're lucky and maybe, just maybe, you'll get a good job. Don't throw your life away. It's not worth it." He stared at her hard. "And whatever you do, watch the company you keep." He turned his attention back to the road, while radioing in Charly's impending arrival to someone at the jailhouse on the other end of the dial.

He made a left, and Charly exhaled. Her feet were hurting, her wrists were burning, and her attitude was on fire. She was pissed beyond pisstivity, and someone was going to pay for it. That someone was Rory.

"So you're still not going to talk to me?" the officer asked.

Charly rolled her eyes. She'd said all she was going to say, which, according to the code she'd been taught by the streets, was too much. Yes, she'd given him some information, but when he pulled out his little notepad and pen, she sealed her lips. When he finished writing, then asked her to sign, she'd refused. That was one autograph that wasn't going to be handed out. There was no way she would ever sign a contract saying she'd stolen a car when she hadn't, at least not to her knowledge or on purpose. When Officer Unfriendly questioned if she understood him, her teachings from Dr. Deveraux El kicked in, and she told him no, then informed him that she stood over him. Her lips spread into a slight smile, she was happy that Dr. Deveraux El had made her research words in the fourth volume of *Black's Law Dictionary,* and now she knew that *understood,* to the law, was akin to a contractual obligation to agree to something. Charly nodded. She wasn't bowing down or signing anything. She wasn't being difficult either, she was just preserving, not reserving her rights. That's why she had nothing to say to the officer; her words wouldn't count anyway. The judge's voice is what mattered. She'd just let the universe take care of it. She knew who she was, and that's all that counted. She wasn't a thief, she was a giver, she reminded herself, then closed her eyes. She saw no sense in witnessing herself going to jail.

She felt the car turn left, zip down the streets, then hang a right. When it slowed, and then stopped, she clenched her teeth. It was time to face a new reality, which meant opening her eyes. As much as she wanted to hide behind her lids, she knew doing so wouldn't erase what was going on. With much effort, she opened them, then stared at the officer through the rearview mirror. "So you think you can take these cuffs off me now? Or are you afraid I'll overpower you and run?" she asked, her tone sarcastic and daring.

He stared at her while grabbing his clipboard from the passenger seat. "You don't have much respect for authority, Charly. Do you?"

With her hands behind her back, she leaned forward. "What's your name?"

"Officer Michaels," he answered, pointing to his badge. "Do you want my badge number too?"

Charly sat back, shaking her head. "No, what I want is for you to stop calling me Charly. You want me to call you Officer Michaels, and think it's okay for you to call me by my first name? Nah. I don't think so. Only I can determine who and what has authority over me, and, in my book, we're equals. As it is above, so it is below," she said.

Officer Michaels gave her a quizzical look. "What does that mean?"

She shook her head. "Do your homework, then you'll see why I stand over you and you'll understand me. For now, let's just say that your job can't put you above me, just as you being an adult doesn't make me less than you because I'm a teenager," she informed him. "So can we respect each other now, or do you plan on continuing to treat me like a criminal before you really know if I'm one?"

He shook his head as if disgusted with her, then got out of the car and slammed the door. He walked toward the back of the vehicle, then made his way behind it. Charly gritted her teeth. It was time to face the drama, and she was ready to get it over with. She sat there for seconds waiting for Officer Unfriendly to release her from the confines of the squad car, but he didn't. In fact, he'd disappeared from view, she discovered as she looked through the front and side windows. She'd just been looking at him, then suddenly it was as if he'd vanished. She blinked twice, hoping her sight was deceiving her, but he was still nowhere to be seen. She tilted her head. How could he have gone missing so quickly? she wondered, closing her eyes, then resting her head on the seat. There was no use in worrying, she told herself. There was no use in rushing; she had nowhere to go but to jail.

Her door opened, jarring her. "Come on. And please watch your head while getting out. I don't want you to get hurt," the officer said. His voice held a different tone. He wasn't outwardly apologetic, but he wasn't as rigid and accusing as before.

Charly lowered her head while getting out of the vehicle. She stiffened when he grabbed her arm, helping her to her feet. "Thank you, I guess." Her words were uncertain. She didn't know if she should be thankful for him not wanting her to get hurt, or be upset that she was handcuffed and on her way to get booked.

"So you are Charly St. James? Huh? Born in Illinois, resident of New York, actress," he said, his words telling her he'd checked her out.

Charly looked at him, and a funny sort of glee replaced her anger. She was having an I-told-you-so moment, and it felt good. "Yes. I am Charly St. James. And you are . . . sorry? Huh?"

Officer Michaels shook his head, then pulled slightly on her arm to guide her into the precinct. "Are all New Yorkers as difficult as you? I heard it's true; now I'm wondering."

Charly laughed. Despite the handcuffs she wore, she still felt good about herself. "New Yorkers difficult?" She shook her head. "Nah. It's not city people who are difficult; it's usually the truth that's difficult. I told you the truth—my honesty was easy—you made the truth difficult." She walked up the two steps that led into the precinct. "Let's get this over with. I have a show to do, and you're holding up our progress."

Finally, he smiled, holding open the door for her. "So I've heard. I guess you really do know the mayor. More importantly, he knows you, and we're going to let you walk. There was no harm done to the car, and no one wants to press charges on someone who came here to do good for the community." He led her into a backroom.

"But I still have to hold you though, until someone comes to claim you."

Charly's eyes lit. She was out of trouble; now she could flip back into her role. She had to save Nia from dreariness, and keep the show interesting. She figured she might as well use jail for more than it was usually worth. "Cool, but I need a favor. Can we tape it? You know, like the whole thing. Maybe we can do a do-over and you can put me back into the car, ride for a couple of blocks, walk me in, etcetera. It'll be good for ratings, and if I can take a few cute mug shots, that'll be great too."

Liam was smiling and leaning against a mailbox when she came out. Her lips spread farther than his, as she skipped down the two steps and made her way over to him.

"Only you, Charly. Only you. How'd you end up in jail?" He shook his head. "Never mind. Dumb question," he said, then nodded slightly to where the cameraman and boom man were standing and filming. Her smile spread wider. The officer wouldn't agree to Charly's request for a go-to-jail do-over, but he'd let her call the crew, and they'd come to her rescue. She may not have gotten it all captured for the show, but she'd take what she could get.

"Liam, please. You already know, but what you don't know is that when I catch Rory, we're going to get it in. I'm talking a real fight. I don't know how I'm going to pull it off because I don't want to get sued," she said, getting ready to cross the street. She stepped off the curb.

Liam pulled her back. "You trying to get run over, love?" He looked at her and winked. "We've got to get over to Nia's, who's finally showed up, by the way, and I can't let anything happen to you beforehand," he said, then whispered, "and after last night, I feel you're my responsibility."

Charly punched him, then caught herself. "Liam! Don't even play like that. That's not cool. You know if someone heard you, that'd blow like gasoline and lit matches." Her words were low and fiery, and also said between clenched teeth.

He held his chest where her fist had just connected. "Ouch! I'm not playing." She cut him a look. "And I don't mean it like that, Charly. I just feel I need to protect you because *someone* knows where you're staying and how to get to you." His tone was different, serious.

She nodded. He had a point, and she was grateful that he had her back. "Thanks," she said to Liam.

"Charly!" someone called, making her and Liam cringe.

They had too much to accomplish and too short of a time to do it in, and, now there just wasn't time to deal with the townspeople. Liam grabbed her hand and pulled her. "C'mon!"

"Hi!" Charly yelled to whomever, then turned to Liam. "Where are we going?"

"You'll see," he said, still pulling her along as the cameraman and boom man followed. Hand in hand, they jogged to a parking lot by the precinct. "Over here," he directed, crossing over the blacktop toward a convertible Mustang.

"Nice. When did you get this?" she asked, rounding to

the passenger side, then bid the cameraman and boom man good-bye as they signaled they were cutting the taping.

"We'll meet you guys back at the location," Liam said to them, then turned his attention back to Charly. "I just picked it up not too long ago. I can't stand being chauffeured around. We need to enjoy ourselves . . . and staying off of the studio's grid—their schedule for us—is priority." He opened her door.

She pressed her lips together, then crinkled her brows. She looked at him when he got in. "But how? You're not old enough to rent a car. Don't you have to be like twenty-something to do that?" Charly strapped in.

Liam got in, put on his seat belt, then started the car. He pressed a button, and the convertible yawned open. "Nice!" he exclaimed, breathing in the fresh air. He revved the engine, and shrugged. "Star power, love. Just using my star power. Sometimes we have to use what we got. I signed a few autographs and did some flirting, and just like that"—he snapped his fingers—"they let me rent it. I have a credit card and I'm licensed, so it's not a big deal really," he said, then pulled off.

11

The sun warmed Charly's face, and her hair danced in the wind as Liam pressed the accelerator. She put on her sunglasses, then reclined her seat. It felt good to have the breeze kiss her face, especially after being held in the police cruiser and sitting in the station. The clean air was refreshing to a city girl, and she marveled at how much she appreciated not having to endure the smoggy gas fumes she'd grown used to in the busy New York traffic. "Now the rest of today's gonna be nice, I can feel it, especially since we have Nia in place," she said to Liam, looking over and giving him a pleasant smile.

He smiled, then slowed the car, and finally came to a stop at a red light. "I hope so, love. 'Cause we've got a lot of work to do, and so little time . . ." he began, then stopped. He grimaced aloud.

"What?" Charly asked, not liking his look.

"Hope your feeling sticks—the nice day part," he mumbled loud enough for her to hear.

"Liam! Liam! I thought that was you. There's this huge party tonight, and everyone's going. I'm running late, and I need to get ready. Can you give me a ride?" a singsong voice sang, growing closer by the second, an indication that she was nearing the car.

"Oh, gawd," Charly whispered, and slumped down farther in her seat. She knew she couldn't escape being seen, but she wanted to. "I've already been with Rory today. I'm not up for Mya and her full-of-her-selfness. Please tell me that's not her."

Liam pasted on a phony smile, and gave a half wave. "I would love to, but I'm afraid it's her," he managed to say between clenched teeth. "Pardon?" he called out to Mya.

"Come on, Mr. I'm Single. You know you wanna give me a ride," rolled out of her mouth in the most flirtatious tone Charly had ever heard, and it sickened her to her stomach. Mya's voice was one of the reasons for Charly's disgust, the other was Mya directly hitting on Liam, who belonged to Charly. At least for television, she reminded herself.

She lifted her sunglasses and gave Liam the side eye. "Disgusting! That's who you were talking to when I was out working trying to get Nia to accept bettering herself?" She lowered her shades and turned her face away. Liam had some nerve flirting with her project's twin sister.

"Well, well . . ." he stammered, and Charly didn't know if he was stumbling for words to answer her or Mya.

"Don't be shy, Liam. You weren't shy the last time we were around each other. Besides, you know you want—oh, I didn't see you in the car, Charly!" Mya said, her voice changed from flirtatious to regret. Probably from being caught flirting, Charly assumed. Her voice was also closer than ever, Charly realized when she turned her head and came face-to-face with the outgoing sister.

Liam drummed on the steering wheel, and Charly tried to determine if it was because of his nerves or impatience. Had he been flirting with Mya or had he wished they hadn't run into her either? she questioned, trying to read him. She looked from him to Mya and back again, and still couldn't determine. "Oh, hi, Mya. Another party, already? Didn't you just go to one?" she greeted in a tone much happier than her true feelings.

"Where do—" Liam began.

"No, I'm doing the talking. I'm responsible for the people; you're responsible for the structure. Remember?" Charly said, cutting him off. Her voice was edgy, and her attitude was serious. "Sorry about that, Mya. It's the rules. Liam's here for building, I'm here for everything else—everyone else." She pasted a phony smile on her face. "So you were saying you need a ride. Where?"

Mya bit her bottom lip and tried to keep a straight face, but was unsuccessful. Charly could see disappointment in her eyes. "It's summer. There's always a party. And this is hands down, the best one of the year. I need a ride to the house . . . if you were going that way, that would be cool."

Charly nodded. "Ah, wouldn't you know it, Mya, that's exactly where we're headed. Hop in," she said, then

looked in the backseat and saw that Liam had some sup-
plies and paperwork there. "One sec," she said, then
pushed herself up and turned around in her seat, then adjusted her body so she could reach Liam's belongings. She
moved them to the side so Mya would have to sit behind
Liam, which was where she needed her to be so she could
keep an eye on her. It bothered her that this girl was
clearly after him, but what got under her skin even more
was that she cared. She wasn't supposed to have real feelings for Liam, and she didn't. That's what she told herself, but she couldn't convince herself of a lie. Liam was
in her system, and that was all there was to it. "Okay,
you can get in now. Everything's out of your way," she
said, then turned back around, and nodded to Liam. She
reached for the stereo system volume, then cranked it.
Mya could ride with them, sure, but she wasn't going to
get any conversation. Especially from Liam. Mya hopped
in and set her purse on the floor. Charly tilted her head
quizzically, then muted the music. "Mya, one thing. Why
are you always riding with someone? Your dad has like a
thousand cars at your house. And Nia drives, so why
don't you?" She threw the question out there, knowing
that Mya did drive. Well, at least Rory said she did, and
Charly had no reason to doubt her.

The blood and expression drained from Mya's face, letting Charly know she'd struck a nerve. "I can't drive" was
all she said before Charly turned up the volume. She refused
to listen to any more lies that came out of Mya's mouth.

Mya was out of the car and in the house before Charly
and Liam could gather their things. Her heart was racing,

knowing she had to move quickly. It had only been a day, and already she was way behind with Nia. Now, without Rory to help her, she didn't know how she was going to reach Nia, but she would.

"Looks like you've got company," Liam said, closing the trunk.

Charly looked over her shoulder and gulped. Nia was standing in the doorway, waving. She looked like a confused farmer, wearing grungy brown overall shorts, complete with shoulder straps, a red and beige checkered top and sandals with two straps. Her hair was pulled back in a crooked ponytail, and her face was dull. Despite her appearance, Charly smiled. She was happy to have her come to greet them. Nia waved harder, then walked over to them. "Need help with anything?" she asked Charly.

Charly gave her a friendly hug, but was careful not to squeeze too tight. Nia didn't seem to be one who was big on affection, so she didn't want to throw her off, especially since she'd come out to meet them. That she'd come without being called or tricked or pressured was a plus. "No, Liam has all the big stuff. I just have my bag. It's good to see you, Nia. So, I guess that means . . . ?"

Nia nodded. "Yes, it means I'm willing to help you help my dad." She rolled her eyes, then nodded her head toward the house. "I'm probably the only one around here who will since my mom is away, and because everyone else will be partying. Seems you have a knack for rubbing people the wrong way. I guess you need to brush up on your kissing-up skills." She laughed a little.

Charly's eyes stretched in surprise. So that was the key, she figured. If one sister helped, the other didn't. Why didn't she see that the other day? she questioned. When Mya was wrapped up in herself and refused to show them out to the pool house, Nia wasn't around. When Mya showed up, Nia disappeared. Mya thought herself superior to her sister, and Nia smiled and offered her help after Charly had rubbed Mya the wrong way, and outright laughed because Charly wasn't a kiss-up. She didn't know if their separation qualified as sibling rivalry or not, but it definitely said they weren't close. "Well, Nia, I guess that means I'll never have any friends, because these lips don't kiss up! Now, are you ready to roll? We gotta shop 'til we drop."

12

Nia whipped the car down the highway, leaving Tallu-lahville and heading toward Minneapolis. Charly cranked up the music, and danced in her seat. She elbowed Nia, urging her to let go and let loose. Nia shook her head and rolled her eyes, then smiled. They turned left, and Charly looked around. Tall buildings, pedestrians, and a traffic jam met her eyes. She exhaled. Seeing a city made her feel at home, and she couldn't wait to get out and into the thick of it.

"Nia?" she asked, turning down the music. "So what's up with the parties? You don't go to any?"

"I've never been the partying type. I've gone a couple of times with Mya, but they weren't for me. As I'm sure you can tell, I'm not exactly the crowd type," she said, heading toward a mall.

Charly gulped. The more she paid attention, the more she learned. So Nia and Mya had partied together before? She never would've guessed it, but she wasn't going to bring it up either. Nia's guard was coming down, and that's exactly where she needed it to be able to get through to her. "So about the not being a crowd type, is that across the board? Or does it apply just some of the time?" she questioned, hoping Nia's dislike for crowds was something she could get her to work through. She needed to reinvent her from the inside out, and that meant she had to get her to lighten up and, possibly, have fun.

Nia smoothed her dull ponytail, then turned into the mall parking lot. She exhaled, an obvious frustration growing in her. "I'm not sure what you're asking, Charly," she said, then whipped the car into a garage adjacent to one of the big stores.

"You know, crowds? Like do you ever do crowds? I mean, personally, I can do without them, but sometimes I have to deal with them. And believe it or not, sometimes I even have a good time."

Nia turned into a stall, put the car in park, and killed the engine. She grabbed her awful-looking purse from the backseat, then looked at Charly. "Well, of course you would say that. Look at you."

After exiting the car and entering the mall, Charly spent the next ten minutes or so pondering Nia's statement. When they walked past a huge storefront window, she compared their appearances in the reflection. She was jazzy and cute, and Nia just was. Nia didn't stand out, and nothing about her said memorable, not in a good way. But she could change that, she was sure. Giving Nia the once-over once more, she knew she had to do something quickly. The girl's style was killing her, and she was clueless about it.

"You mind if we go into the bookstore?" Nia asked, wearing a hopeful look. "I know we're here for my dad, and I promise you there's a couple of good stores here, and some really nice high-end furniture places on the strip, but there's a book I must have."

Charly pasted on a smile. She'd give Nia anything she wanted to get what she wanted from her. She just had to figure out how to make her give in because Nia wasn't going to do it willingly. "Cool. Lead the way."

As soon as they entered the bookstore, Nia tensed and began to fidget. "You know what, Charly? Never mind. We're supposed to be here for my dad, so my book can wait," she said to Charly, turning around.

Charly looked over Nia's shoulder, and her eyes lit. Trent was nearby, holding a book in his hand. She tilted her head and focused her eyes to be sure it was him, but she didn't have to. Nia's demeanor and nervousness confirmed it for her. "Oh, isn't that Trent over there?" she asked, playing dumb. "We should go say hi."

Nia's eyes stretched, then she looked down at her clothes, which told Charly she was more aware of her dowdiness than she'd let on. "No, that's okay. He's busy, and we have stuff to do."

Charly shook her head, then grabbed Nia by the forearm. "Come on. We don't wanna be rude. He did offer to help, after all." She took two steps, then was snatched back, hard and quickly. Nerdy or not, Nia was strong.

"No," she snapped in a loud whisper, pulling Charly out of the store, and releasing her from her grip. Her answer was clipped and emphatic, and her expression was just as hard.

Charly stood to the side, and crossed her arms. She tapped her foot and smiled like a Cheshire cat. With tilted head, she asked, "Why not? What's so wrong with saying hello? I mean, if you don't like him . . . Right? You said you don't like him," Charly pushed. It didn't matter what Nia said with words, she did like Trent. A lot. Anyone who had sight could tell that. "So, I'll just go say hello."

Nia grimaced and grabbed her arm. Her look was serious and cold . . . and revealing. This side of Nia wasn't shy or meek, but mean. "I said no." Charly raised her brows and squared her shoulders. Nia could get as mad as she wanted; it didn't faze her. She'd gone up against worse, namely the incident with the police and Rory. She still hadn't forgotten about that, and couldn't wait to connect her fist with Rory's lying mouth that sent her to jail.

Charly stared at her, then looked down to where Nia's hand was. She cleared her throat, and Nia let her go.

As if she hadn't just snapped and snatched Charly's arm, Nia batted her eyes 'til they teared up. Seeing Nia's mood switch so quickly, Charly began to wonder which was off: Nia's emotional stability or her sincerity. "Please?" Nia pleaded. "Not like this." She pulled on her clothes.

Charly's eyebrows rose and she let go of her suspicions for a moment. She had Nia right where she wanted her. "I got'cha, but you're gonna have to do something for me for me to do this—or rather, not do this—for you."

"What?" Nia sounded scared and uncertain.

Charly exhaled. "You have to give me two full days."

Nia shrugged. "I can do that. It's for my father—"

"No." Charly stopped her. "Two days of helping you help yourself. I mean, look at you, Nia. There we were on your playground—the bookstore—and you couldn't even play because you're not comfortable with yourself. You're smart. I'm sure somewhere deep down you're probably witty, too." Nia's face went blank. "Okay, maybe not, but still. You're a nerd—the smartest girl in school, I bet."

"The smartest girl in the county and, last I heard, the state," Nia corrected. "But smart doesn't matter, unless you count the universities that only want to use you."

Charly tilted her head. "Use you how?"

Nia turned her face away. "They only want you because you'll make their stats look good. I know that's why they came after me after I took the pre-SATS a few years ago. Ever since then, they won't stop. They keep hounding and scouting and recruiting. So who does smart really matter for?"

Charly grabbed Nia's shoulders. "Are you freakin' kidding me? 'Smart doesn't matter'? It does matter. It makes the world go 'round. So my question to you is why not be the best at it? If you're gonna be a nerd, be the best nerd there is—period. Handle your position, master it like the Google and Facebook guys and Bill Gates."

Nia was stuck on stupid, and didn't speak for seconds. "But how, Charly? Mya's the one everybody—"

"Forget Mya. I'm talking about you, Nia. And to answer your question *how*, you're looking at how." She held out her arms and turned around in a complete circle, then nodded her head in a so-there fashion. "Nia, let's just have fun. Everything else will come together." Charly's cell phone vibrated, interrupting her speech. She looked at the screen and saw she had a text message from a blocked number. She shrugged and opened it. A bag of Skittles appeared on the screen with the same warning: YOU'RE BEING PLAYED.

13

They sat on Nia's bed sorting clothes in two stacks. Charly had managed to walk away with five pair of shoes, three for Nia, who didn't suspect it, and two for herself. She'd also bought bags and bags of clothes and, thanks to Nia's insistence, several books on cracking calculus and improving her vocabulary. She'd protested at first, and had taken it as a jab against her smarts, then appreciated Nia's advice. Statistics had proven that people with a broader lexicon, word knowledge, and command, were more respected and paid higher. Charly could live with that, she told herself. Who didn't want respect and more pay? Plus, mastering words would prepare her for the GRE before college, and there was nothing like being ahead, Nia had told her. Being a frontrunner had already given Nia a list of scholarships to choose from. Charly looked at her project, and began to see her as a person, not a thing she had to fix. True, their looks were different. Charly sparkled like a diamond and Nia resembled dust. But Charly knew that the girl sitting before her was a gem just waiting to be cleaned so she could gleam. Her personality, that was finally surfacing, was also warm and infectious.

"So . . . you're really going to wear these?" Nia asked, holding up a pair of four-inch heels.

Charly laughed. "Yes, of course, and they're gonna be hot too."

Nia shook her head and put down the shoes. "They'll be hot for you, but would be pain for me." She picked up another pair that was barely two inches high. "These too. I could never walk in these."

Charly gagged. Surely Nia was kidding. She was seventeen, her shoe skills should've been inherent by now. "Don't tell me you can't walk in heels. That's so . . . so cliché for a nerd. If you can walk with all those books I'm sure you carry around, you should be able to glide in heels. It's just balancing a different part of your body."

Nia shook her head. "Yeah, right."

Charly moved one of the piles of clothes out of her way, then got off the bed. She walked over to one of the bookcases, then took down several big books. "Come on," she beckoned Nia. "Grab a pair of shoes."

Nia was still shaking her head. She burst out laughing. "No. No. No. I know everyone thinks I'm sullen, but I'm not suicidal. Any of these shoes would result in death from breaking my neck."

Charly set the heavy books down on the desk, and put

her hand on her hip. "C'mon. Grab a pair. I bet you fifteen dollars that I can turn you into catwalk material in under an hour."

Nia was wiping tears from her eyes because she'd laughed herself to tears. "Thirty, and you've got a deal." She nodded. "Which pair?"

Charly smiled. "The universe blessed us to wear the same size, so you choose. Just make sure it's a high pair," Charly urged.

With hesitancy and a purposefully loud moan, Nia selected a pair of three-inch heels, then Charly shook her head no. Nia shrugged, then picked up the highest ones on the bed, which were a whopping five inches high, but had a forgiving one-inch platform under the front of the shoes. "If I'm going to risk my life, I might as well get it over with quickly," she said, then slipped off her sandals and began putting on the five-inchers.

"That's my girl. Go hard or go home," Charly said, walking over to Nia to help her to her feet.

Nia's legs shook, and her ankles wobbled. For a second, Charly thought she was going to lose the bet, but she couldn't let that happen. She was a go-getter not a quitter, plus winning the thirty bucks would be great because the studio wasn't going to reimburse her for her things. Nia was the recipient of the goods. "Wait. Wait. Wait . . ." she instructed. "Hold on to my shoulders. Spread your feet shoulder-width apart. Now lock your knees. Hold it. Don't move," she said, then hustled over to the desk and grabbed the stack of heavy books. She lugged them back over to where Nia was standing, set them on the mattress, then climbed on top of it. Nia was towering over her, and there was no way she could stack the books on Nia's head while standing on the floor. "Still. Be perfectly still, Nia." She put two encyclopedias on Nia's head, followed by a dictionary and *The Complete Works of William Shakespeare*. "Give me your hands. Now hold these in place while I get down," she instructed, first positioning Nia's hands correctly, then getting off the bed.

Nia stood there looking like the Chiquita Banana woman from back in the day, balancing stuff on her head. Charly walked in front of her, then held out one hand to Nia. "Shouldn't I practice walking without the books first?"

"Look, stay in your lane and let me handle mine. You're great at schoolwork, I'm spectacular at fashion. Now balance the books with one of your hands and give me the other. Think of it as a different sort of physics. You're going to think about the books not falling. That's it." Charly took Nia's hand, and began walking backward, inches at a time. Nia wobbled and froze, then exhaled. The look on her face was determined, and Charly was proud.

First she took tiny steps, then gradually moved into a slow stride. The books almost fell, but Nia let go of Charly's hand, then reached up with both of hers and held them in place. Before they knew it, she'd walked across the room and back more times than they could count. Nia smiled big and wide. "I got it. I got it, Charly!"

Charly nodded, then held out her hand. "I was counting on it. Thirty big ones right here, please." She wiggled her fingers on her outstretched palm.

The door burst open. "Nia? What are you doing? I know *you're* not in heels!" Mya asked, crossing her arms. Her lips poked out, and her eyebrows were raised in judgment.

The books fell off Nia's head and onto the floor with a loud thud. And though Charly couldn't hear it, she knew Nia's pride had followed suit. "I . . . uh . . ." Nia stammered. She forced a barely there smile, then reached down and began unbuckling the shoes. She slipped them off one at a time. She rolled her eyes at herself. "I know, right? I don't wear stuff like this. Charly and I had a bet. That's it. You know fashion isn't my thing." She looked up and shrugged before standing. "Charly, Mya's the fashion diva in the family. She's like the high-heel expert around here. I bet she'd take your money because she can jog in stilettos." Her praise for her twin sister was genuine, but her voice was filled with regret.

Charly looked from one twin to the other, and noticed the huge difference. It wasn't their opposite tastes in fashion, or the scar zigzagging down Nia's face, and she knew it wasn't the popular sister versus the nerdy sister that separated them either. That couldn't be it. From the yearbook pictures she'd seen of Mya, Mya was once just as nerdy and unappealing as Nia. She wondered when that had taken place and what caused Mya's change. Her gut told her Mya's blossoming had something to do with one sibling being clearly dominant over the other. Maybe Mya felt prettier and, thus, more deserving. Charly didn't have her whys lined up, but she would. Whatever it was she'd get down to it, she had to. "Hmph," she said, watching the interaction between the two. Nia's bowing down to Mya, and Mya relishing in her power, exerting it like someone had made her queen told Charly if she wanted to help Nia, she'd have to first get to Mya. Mya was the wall that barricaded Nia in her shell, and Charly had to figure out why Mya was so angry. Why was she passive aggressively bullying her twin sister? Getting to the thick of it was going to be rough, she knew, because she didn't care for Mya.

Mya smiled, then went and picked up the shoes. "Oh, these are superhot." She started kicking off her flip-flops, apparently getting ready to try on the high heels.

Charly walked over to her, then reached for the shoes. "Sorry, Mya. Nia was just breaking them in. They're mine." Charly scrunched her nose, took the heels, then reached in her pocket and retrieved some money. She peeled off a few bills, then handed them to Nia. "You won. I bet you couldn't break them in." She held up a shoe, then looked at it. "And I lost. No more gambling for me."

Nia looked appreciative, and Mya looked scorned. Charly went over to the bed, and began refilling the shopping bags from the mall. There was no way she was going to allow Mya to get to the rest of the shoes and gear. Sure, ninety-nine percent of it was for Nia, but Nia didn't know. She'd played the sidelines, waiting in chairs while Charly shopped. Charly only hoped the clothes fit properly. Nia had told her her sizes the first day they'd met, but Charly knew for a fact that many girls lied about their size because she sometimes did. "Okay, ladies, I've wasted too much time. I have to get back to work," she fibbed, excusing herself. The bags banged against her leg as she walked out. It took everything within her not to slam the door behind her. Mya—her entitlement and passive bullying of Nia—got under Charly's skin.

"Hi, Charly," Trent greeted, surprising her on her way down the stairs.

Charly stopped, and talked herself down. She was barely seconds away from making a U-turn and going back to snatch Mya off her high post. Now she had to calm herself because she wasn't there to hand out butt kickings, but she wasn't beyond doing so either. "Oh, hi, Trent," she replied. "It's good to see you. You on your way to see Nia?" she quizzed, waiting to read his expression.

He froze, then shook his head in the negative. His pregnant pause told Charly he wasn't as against the idea of Nia as he was pretending to be. "Um, no. I was just going to the rest room."

Charly smiled. "Trent, this isn't my business, but you know that I know that this house has many bathrooms. There's even one outside, and a couple downstairs, right?"

Trent nodded. "Yeah, I guess."

"Well, so that must mean one of two things: you prefer the bathroom up here or you're stalking Mya. I mean, since you aren't interested in Nia," Charly said, her expression knowing, daring him to be honest.

Trent reared back his head as if he were dodging a physical blow. "Mya? Are you kidding me?" He laughed. "You've got me all wrong. I'm not into . . . Well, never mind. It was good seeing you, Charly. Can you tell Liam

I'll be right back? He's gonna show me how to make some precision cuts on one of the power saws."

"Will do, Trent. I'll see you outside." She began walking down the stairs.

"And later too, right? At the party? Liam promised you guys would be there."

Charly just looked at him and smiled. There was no way she was going to agree, and she wouldn't turn him down either. She had some thinking and scheming to do, and she didn't know what would work in her favor. She was certain of one thing, though. There was no way Liam would be attending any party without her, especially if Mya was going to be there.

14

——————

Charly almost ran to get out of the house. She couldn't get to Liam fast enough. It was bad enough she had to deal with the fluctuating attitudes of Nia and Mya, now she was supposed to party with the locals too? No, she thought not. She pushed through the back door, then speed walked toward the pool house. The backyard was quickly turning into a set. Tables were up, tools were arriving, and tents were leaned against the house, waiting to be pitched.

"Hey, Charly, can you pose for a picture?" someone asked.

Charly looked to her right, noticing a familiar face. She couldn't remember where she knew him from, but she was certain she did. "Sure. I'd love to . . . ?" She left her uncertainty hanging in the air for him to grab and answer, but he didn't.

"Thanks," he said, walking over and standing next to her. He wrapped one arm around her, pulled her in tight, then held up his cell phone in front of them. "Okay. One. Two. Three. Get ready," he said, pressing the phone until a shutter sound could be heard.

"Please don't take this the wrong way because I'm not trying to push up on you or anything, but I know that I know you from somewhere. Don't I?" she had to ask between smiles while he took more pictures of them. It wasn't that she was interested in him; she just had to know if they'd met before, for a couple of reasons. One, he was kind of cute, but not exactly her type. Still, she never forgot a handsome face, or at least tried not to. Two, if he was some newbie to the show who she'd seen in passing, she had to worry. If he was there from New York, that meant the rest of the *Extreme Dream Team* crew was there too, and that meant her time had pretty much run out. She pursed her lips together, hoping he wasn't with the network. They'd given her days to begin her mission, and she'd hate for them to go back on their word, especially because Nia was turning out to be a tougher project than she'd expected.

"Mitch! Hey, Mitch!" someone was yelling in a loud voice that was so squeaky it could only belong to one person. A girl whose head needed splitting, as far as Charly was concerned.

Rory? Charly turned her head, trying to see the person the voice belonged to. She was sure it was Rory, but she had to be sure before she walked over there and bashed the wrong person in the face. She stretched her neck, looking in the direction from which the voice came, but couldn't get a view of the girl.

"One sec," the guy replied back, telling Charly he was obviously Mitch. "You must've met my younger brother, Mike. Our genes are strong, but I don't think we look that much alike. Everyone says so though. Our names being similar doesn't help too much either."

Charly tilted her head. "So does everyone here know everyone else?"

"Mitch, hurry up. I gotta go get my pretty on before the party," Rory was now yelling from the other side of the pool.

"Rory! Wait. Wait right there," Charly said, disconnecting herself from the conversation with Mitch. She turned, then walked as fast and hard as she could to get to Rory. She'd promised herself that her fist was going to connect with Rory's jaw as soon as she saw her, and now her hand was itching to make the connection. Charly balled her hand, then released her fingers in a stretch. As she was making a fist again, a hand was on her arm, yanking her back.

"Charly, love. Where are you going? I need you over here," Liam said, jumping in front of her. His hand was still on her arm, and he was smiling, but it was forced.

Charly, not appreciating being jerked around, shot him a nasty look. "If you don't get your hand off me, Liam, I'm going to knock *you* out first. Straight up, no chaser other than my foot. Got it?"

Liam didn't budge. His gaze bore into Charly's eyes with a look more serious than she'd ever seen him wear before. "I'm not letting you kill your career or mine, for

that matter," he said, pulling her back, and almost dragging her to the pool house.

Reluctantly, Charly followed. Really, she had no choice.
Liam was strong, and he was also determined, she realized. With a hand still on her arm, he opened the door,
and all but pushed her inside. He closed them inside, then
released her.

"You didn't have to—" she began.

"Yes, I did. What's your problem? It's like you're mad
at the world. Is it like your time of the month or something?" He held up his hand, then spread his fingers, one
at a time with each point. "You don't like Mya, the girl at
the hotel, now Rory. Who's next—me?"

Charly ground her feet into the floor to keep her balance, then shoved him. "Serious? I mean, serious? Why
does it always have to be a girl's time of the month if
she's upset? You guys don't know jack about women."
She rolled her eyes. "Why don't you try going over the
list again, Liam?" She put a finger in the air. "One,
Heaven—that's the hotel chick—is awful, and you know
it. She's rude. Two, Rory got me locked up, Liam! She
lied. Point-blank and period. It wasn't her car and she
didn't have permission. Now, had she told me, you guys
wouldn't have been picking me up from the station," she
snapped, raising another finger in the air. "And don't let
me even begin to tell you about Ms. I'm So Fantastic
Mya. She's full of herself, thinks her ish doesn't stink, and
I really think she's some sort of bully. And . . . and . . ."
She was reaching for the other things she didn't like, but
couldn't find the words.

"And she's after me," Liam said, deadpanning her.

"You're jealous, Charly St. James. You think you have competition, and it's killing you. Go on and admit it. You don't like Mya because you think Mya likes me," he stated matter-of-factly, crossing his arms.

"Pssh." Charly blew him off with a sound. She rolled her eyes again. "Whatever. Try again, Liam. You're great to look at and nice and toned and tall and smart. You're a lot of positives, but so am I. So, really, it's not that serious."

Liam laughed. "But it is, love. It is that serious," he said, his voice lowering. His eyes sparkled as he looked at her. It was the same look he'd given her the season before, the time when he kissed her and bought her her favorite dessert.

Charly's knees started weakening, her heart sped, and her mouth was going dry. She swallowed, heard a gulping sound, and prayed Liam didn't. The pool house was big inside, airy, and tastefully decorated, but suddenly it felt small and as if it were sucking all the wind out of her. She pushed past Liam. "I was breaking the barrier with Nia, then that was ruined by Mya who, by the way, I'm going to have to connect with to accomplish the mission. Ugh! And you won't let me beat down Rory, and I'm not working on designing or building the new room for Nia today. So that means my job is done here. Anything else I need to do, I can do in my room."

Liam licked his lips. "If you just hold on for a while, I'll be ready."

Charly shook her head. There was no way she was giving him the opportunity to see her swoon anymore. She'd been too transparent as it was with him hearing her gulp, and was sure she had started sweating from the rapid beating of her heart. It'd been drumming so quickly, she was certain it had her in cardiovascular mode. "Thanks, but no thanks. I'm ready to skate now. I'm sure either the cameraman or the boom guy will drop me off. So I guess I'll meet you at the hotel or just see you tomorrow." She threw up the peace sign, then left.

She and the bed were becoming one. That's what it felt like, and she welcomed it. Her laptop was open on one side of her, her powered-off phone was on the other, and she was resting her forehead on the sketchbook she'd been outlining in. She was only going to close her eyes for two minutes, that's what she'd promised herself before she gave in to the nap that was calling her. Charly pulled the book from under her head, then turned on her side. She had no idea what time it was, and she didn't care. Her day had been long. First she awoke to Liam in her room, then she'd gone through the pits of the underworld just to get a ride from Heaven, only to end up in jail, then had shopped until she copped the right foot wear and clothes that Nia never had a chance to rock because of Mya. She exhaled, releasing the stress. Being a reality star was hard work. "Only one hour, then I'll get back to it," she promised herself, then faded to black.

"Up, Charly. It's time to go," Liam said, his voice sounding real. Even while she was asleep, he was making her weak, and it bothered her. He'd somehow invaded her dream, and she wondered if she could make him go away; that's what she'd heard about lucid dreams. They could be controlled.

"Disappear, Liam!" she demanded, hugging the pillow.

"Love, it's time," he said, his accent sounding more clear and delicious with each word, as if he were next to her.

Charly moaned, then stretched. If she woke up, he'd disappear. She opened her eyes and, sure enough, there he was. She looked at him. She didn't know how he'd gotten in her room, and was too tired to ask. She closed her lids. She'd inquire later.

"Up, love. Up." His tone and inflection only beautified his pronunciation.

His hand was on her shoulder now, moving her side to side. "Time's ticking, love. The party begins in a few, and we can't be late."

Charly's eyes shot open. "What? What about the party? That's the pass."

Liam laughed. "No passes, love. You can't be excused from your own party."

Charly sat up. "What? *My* party?" She looked at him like he had three heads.

He smiled. "The town teens are hosting a bash to thank us."

"That's backward. We haven't done anything yet," she protested. Her arms were still wrapped around the pillow.

His look said he was guilty before his mouth did. Liam shrugged. "Well, we kind of said we'd be there. I couldn't help it, Charly. I agreed, then thought better of it. I even tried to come up with an excuse. I also called you to help me think of something so we could get out of it, but your phone sent me straight to voice mail. But it gets worse."

"Camera coverage?" she asked.

Liam shrugged. "I don't think so, but who knows? The studio called, and said we should attend. And as you know, *should* isn't a suggestion. On the bright side, I'm sure Mya will be there. You said you need to connect with her, so this is your opportunity."

15

Lights were strung in the trees, and lit tiki torches, high up on poles, outlined the backyard of an old bar that'd been converted to an under-twenty-one club named the Juice Pub in the next town. Charly walked carefully on the gravel walk that led to the wooden gate on the side of the building. She was trying to escape and not scuff her heels. She'd been there only three minutes, and was ready to go. There was just too much noise, too much commotion and, to her surprise, too much drinking. It was if she'd entered the teen *Twilight Zone,* where it was cool for teenagers to spike their drinks. She hadn't necessarily seen anyone do it. In fact, many didn't smell of alcohol, but they were acting like they were under the influence.

"Charly? Where are you going? You just got here." Mya's voice caught her before she could escape through the gate.

Charly bit her lip and tried to think of something nice to say to Mya. If she was going to accomplish her goal of transforming Nia, she needed to figure out what the deal was between her and her twin. But she didn't need to sort all that out tonight. "It's not really my type of thing, Mya. Plus, I have to get to work on the sketches for your dad's new digs. I'm sure you understand."

Mya shook her head, walking over to Charly. "No, I don't. I don't really get what's going on." She shrugged, holding a red plastic cup in her hand as if she were about to make a toast, then she gulped from it. She wiped her mouth with the back of her hand, making Charly wonder what was in it. "So why are you here, really? It can't be for my dad—he's loaded. He doesn't need the show to fix up his office."

Charly smiled. "No, he doesn't. But as mayor, it wouldn't look good for him to fix up his own place, then use it for political business. The taxpayers may think he'll use their money to compensate himself. I think that's a crime."

Mya nodded and her face lit. "I never thought about that. Good catch."

"Yes, and the last thing your family needs is more negative publicity," a male voice said, followed by its owner, Trent, who'd appeared out of the darkness.

Charly jumped and held her heart. Mya laughed, then reached in her pocket and pulled out an empty bag of Skittles. She held it in the air. "Well?" she said to Trent.

Charly's antennae went up. What was up with this town and Skittles? "Well?" Charly asked, too.

Trent shook his head, and a look of disbelief covered his face. "Wrong brother, Mya. And you guys promised . . ."

He looked at Charly as if seeing her for the first time, then shut up. She noticed that his eyes said so much more than hello, and so did his answer. "I think Rory's looking for you. She mentioned something about a yellow dress, and there isn't a yellow dress, is it?"

Mya lit, then gulped from her cup again. "Maybe," she sang. "Yellow's my favorite color." She cheesed at Trent, winking, then turned to Charly. "What about you, Charly? You want some candy?"

The yellow dress comment went over Charly's head, and she gritted her teeth at the mention of Rory's name, but smiled. She had to mask her anger and get in Mya's good graces to figure out the wedge between the twins. She also had to find out what "wrong brother" had to do with candy. It was all so weird to her. "Thanks, but no thanks. I need to put something else in my stomach first, like food," she said, meaning it. She hadn't eaten, and sweets were the last thing on her mind. Especially since she could smell barbeque wafting through the yard. "I'll catch up with you after I eat," she promised Mya. "And please don't let Rory leave. I have a surprise for her."

"Cool. I like surprises and so does Rory. I won't spoil it for her though. I promise, and I'll save you some candy," she said to Charly, then turned to Trent. "See ya, wrong brother." She held up the red cup as if saluting him, laughed, then disappeared.

Trent raised his brows, put his hands in his pockets, and rocked on his feet. He had something to say, but wasn't talking. "So?"

Charly parroted him. "So? What?" she asked, then

walked down the gravel path, headed toward the rest of the partygoers in search of the food that was calling her.

Trent jumped right in step with her. "So, I didn't peg you for a candy type of girl."

Charly eyed him, then looked down at herself. She was in shape, but she wasn't so small that she looked hungry. "Myth, Trent. All actresses don't starve themselves. I can eat anything I want, and I usually do." She winked, then zigzagged her way through a throng of teenagers, who seemed either high on a caffeine buzz, quiet like they were sleepwalking, or outright loud and obnoxious like they had something ultrapotent in their cups. "What's up with everybody? And I didn't know you had a brother."

Trent laughed, then held up two fingers. "Two brothers. Mitch and Mike."

Charly nodded. "Oh, if they are who I think they are, then I've met them both. Mike works at the hotel, right? And Mitch was at the house earlier. We took pictures together. They both seem like nice guys. So, you didn't answer my question. What's up with everybody? Something seems off."

Trent paused, then looked at her. "I thought you were a city girl. Aren't you New Yorkers supposed to be up on everything?" He resumed walking, pointing to the other side of the yard.

Charly strolled alongside him. She excused herself after stepping on someone's foot, even though they didn't seem to notice that she'd just about pierced their shoe with her heel. "That's what they say, but I'm not a native New Yorker, and I'm too busy to keep up with *every*thing. So what exactly am I missing?"

Trent excused their way through groups of bystanders who were blocking the makeshift buffet that had a huge spread of food. He pointed to a plate. "I'll fix your plate for you, cool? You're a guest." Charly nodded. He picked it up, then began piling the offerings on it that she agreed to. "You're not missing anything. Trust me. Just eat this." He handed her the plate. "Enjoy the party, and be aware of the *seems*—everyone and everything are not always what they seem. Make sure you stay away from Mya. Rory, too." He walked away, and disappeared into the crowd.

Everything isn't always what it seems, rattled her. It may have not been word for word, but that's exactly what was written on the empty Skittles wrapper someone had slid under her door. Now she wondered if it was Trent. She shook her head, thinking that would be too obvious. If he was going to be sneaky, then he'd be just that. Who'd do something so slick just to give themselves away? She grabbed a piece of chicken, then held her plate in the other hand while she ate. Within seconds, she found her way to a nearby café table, sat down, and began to scarf down her food. Her empty stomach was thanking her with each bite, and so was her tongue as she licked the barbeque sauce off her fingers.

"Wow, love. I've never seen you tear into grub like that!" Liam said, pulling out a chair across from hers. He sat down, then began watching her, making her uncomfortable.

She looked at him, and was glad that she was pretty much finished with her food. If he had joined her two minutes earlier, she wouldn't have been able to eat in peace, not with him staring at her the way he was, and that wouldn't have been good. He slid a cup in front of her. Charly looked at the red plastic tumbler, then up to him. "What's this?"

"Something to drink. I noticed you didn't have anything, so being the gentleman that I am, I brought you something."

Charly picked up the cup and smelled the contents. "What is it? I don't smell anything." The way everyone around them were acting, she sure didn't want what they had in their cups.

"You think I'd do something to you?" Liam laughed, then turned serious when she didn't join him. "It's bottled water. I took it out of one of the coolers, cracked it open, and poured it myself. What's wrong?"

Charly sat back in her seat, then took a long drink. "Do you not see the way they are acting around here? It's like everyone is drunk or high or something."

Liam nodded. "Yes, I noticed. That's why I'm only drinking water that I can open, and if the cap doesn't crack when I twist it—proving it hasn't been opened— I'm not messing with it." The music switched to hip-hop. " 'Ey, that's that old Common song, 'Announcement.' C'mon. We came here to have some fun, so let's get it in," he said, getting out of his seat, then going to help her up from hers. "Let's show them what you've got, Charly St. James. Show them you're more than a pretty face and a tiny waist."

Charly put down her cup, then laughed. They danced their way to the middle of the backyard, and tried to blend in. The plan didn't work, she realized when the other teens surrounded them. A huge smile spread on her face when she looked at Liam. He may've been from overseas, but he could dance. The track switched to a Young Money track, and Charly urged everyone to join them. It was weird having all eyes on them, and she felt like she'd get off beat from all the attention. Liam turned around, and Charly rocked with him from behind.

"Charly, do you mind?" a girl asked.

Charly looked at her and smiled. She didn't want to leave Liam hanging out there, but her feet needed a break. "No, not at all. C'mon," she said, moving out of the way so the girl could take her place. "Where's the ladies' room?" she asked her.

The girl pointed to the pub. "Inside and across the room. You can't miss it. Look for the pink fluorescent light."

"Thanks," Charly said, then trekked across the yard as quickly as she could. As soon as she'd said ladies' room, her bladder seemed anxious. In seconds, she'd made her way to the pub and was opening the door when she saw Rory walking across the open space and going inside a different room. "Yes. I can knock out two things with one trip. First the bathroom, then Rory," Charly said to herself. She couldn't wait to put Rory on her back.

16

There was a lot of racket coming from what appeared to be a private back room, and just as much noise came from all the people in the pub area, who were surrounding a juice bar situated under a sign that read JUICE ONLY—NO ALCOHOL. Charly looked for the neon pink sign that spelled ladies' room, but one wasn't there. What she did see, she didn't like. Over a doorway in the back, huge electric fuchsia letters said SQUATTERS, THIS WAY→, and in blue lettering ←STANDERS, THIS WAY. Charly shook her head. She guessed she was supposed to go toward the right to squat because how dare she just go to the girl's bathroom like a normal girl?

On her way toward the light, she stopped. The noise from inside the closed-off room down the hall from the rest rooms was calling her. Blending in with the rest of the people, she made her way to the door, happy there was a small peephole in it. On tiptoe, she pressed her eye over the hole, trying to see inside. Everything was minimized. She pushed harder, focusing. Things were smaller, but she could make out the crowd and the surroundings. They were encircling a table that held a bowl on top, but she couldn't see what was in it. Whatever it was, though, seemed to be holding their interest, but not hers. Standing on her toes made the bathroom urge return; she began to dance in place.

"Hey! The bathroom's over there," a male bystander said, lingering behind her, obviously waiting to go into the back room. "I do the same thing when I gotta go. I guess everyone has a potty dance."

Charly blushed. She didn't realize that she was being so obvious. She stepped out of his way. "Thanks," she said, then began to walk away.

"Don't worry," he said to her, making her stop and turn around. "Just about everybody came up on a good lick—I'm sure everybody's cabinets are empty—so, believe me, there's plenty left. You're welcome to come in and partake, so hurry back. I'll make sure there's a good variety to choose from, if the spread is as great as it was." He winked.

She didn't know what he was talking about, what "spread" he was referring to. Not knowing what to say, and needing to get rid of the heat her bladder was causing, Charly just winked back. Her feet were connecting with the sticky tiled floor as she sped toward the Squatters sign.

Inside, all she saw were stalls, and as she made her way to them, she noticed they were filled. She grimaced and danced in place. Finally, someone wheeled their wheelchair out of the back one, and Charly brushed past her. She didn't care that she wasn't technically handicapped. Midsquat, she smiled. The sign for the ladies' room may've been a bit crass, but it was definitely befitting because there was no way she was sitting on a public toilet, even if there were paper covers.

"Mya, sister girl, I'm telling you. They don't know me. I just outran my aunt shooting at me, so why would I be scared of anything?" a squeaky voice said.

Charly clenched midstream, and made her stomach knot up. She thought the voice belonged to Rory, but the rush of splashing water was too loud to be sure.

Mya laughed. "Rory, you're crazy. You know that, right?"

Charly let go, rushing herself. She had to hurry up so she could put her hands on Rory. There was no Liam to stop her. No cameras to tape her. There was nothing but a small space and ample opportunity.

"Yes, so I've heard," Rory said. "So what's up with you and Mitch?" she was asking Mya when Charly finished relieving herself, then stood to adjust her clothes.

"Mitch? Mitch? Mitch?" Mya tsked. "Never mind Mitch, ask me about Liam. I don't want local. I want worldwide."

Charly's adrenaline really rose now. She knew Mya was after Liam, but she also knew she wouldn't get him. After zipping her pants, she pulled back her hair and tied it in a knot. She didn't care if her hands weren't clean. Cleanliness wasn't on her mind now. With her foot, she flushed the toilet, then she walked out of the stall.

"Charly!" Mya said, her face a mixture of surprise and

something else. Her look didn't say you've-caught-me this time, it registered that she was under the influence.

" 'Ey, sister girl," Rory began.

Charly knew it was going to happen, but she didn't see it happening. She never saw her fist connect with Rory's face. She turned a blind eye to swinging her fists and kicking her legs. Even putting Rory into a headlock had somehow avoided her view. No, she couldn't see, and she was too mad to feel, but her adrenaline made her act. It pushed her to limits she didn't know she could reach, and made her bounce back when Rory retaliated. It was a fight of the fittest and, to Charly's surprise, it wasn't an easy one.

"Stopitstopitstopit," Mya was yelling while she tried to part them. "Stop!"

Hands were still swinging. Feet were still kicking. Charly's hair was somehow wound around Rory's fist, and the back of Rory's shirt was pulled up and over the front of her head. Charly couldn't move her head and Rory couldn't stand. They'd deadlocked, and unless one of them let the other go, the fight was over.

"That's enough! Just let go. Somebody let go," Mya was still yelling.

"On the count of three," Rory said, her face toward the floor. "You let me go, and I'll let you go."

Charly just heaved. She was tired and out of breath, but she was no fool. There was no way she was going to release Rory from her grip. As long as she had Rory bent over, she could knee her in the face. That was exactly what she was going to do if Rory didn't let her hair go. She was going to break Rory's nose with one swift movement of her leg. As if reading Charly's mind, Rory tightened the hold on Charly's hair, pulling her face closer to hers and making her head turn in an awkward position.

Mya stuck her leg between Charly's leg and Rory's face, then used both her hands to try to untangle Charly's from Rory's shirt and Rory's from Charly's hair. "Come on. Stop. The fight is over," Mya said.

"You better get your hands off me, Charly," Rory demanded.

Charly's laugh was laced with anger. "Or what? You gonna hurt me? How are you gonna do that, because, as you can tell, it won't be with your hands. I guess you're gonna get me locked up again."

"Is that what this is about?" Rory asked, her voice bouncing off the floor.

"What else would it be about?" Charly snapped.

Rory released Charly's hair, then burst out laughing, Now Charly knew for a fact that Rory was crazy. To Charly's surprise, Rory put up her hands in surrender. "You got it. I deserved it."

Charly couldn't believe Rory was mature enough to accept being wrong. The girl was loud and crass and ghettofied, but she was certainly more honest than many, to a degree. There was still the jail thing hanging over her head. Charly stood still for a few seconds, then freed Rory. She jumped back to give herself enough distance to attack again just in case.

Rory looked at Charly with glassy eyes, and Rory smiled. She straightened out her messy hair, nodding her head. "Charly St. James, sister girl! I gotta give it to you. Your little light in the behind butt can scrap. I don't remember ever having a fight like that," she said, slurring her words.

Mya laughed. "That's because no one will fight you, Rory. So, really, it's not that you don't remember. It's that you haven't had one." She grabbed her stomach, then bent over in a fit of laughter. One that was too extreme for the situation.

Charly just stood there taking it all in. Deserving of a butt kicking or not, Rory's reaction was off, and Mya's overwhelming glee made no sense. She sniffed the air expecting the smell of alcohol, but there wasn't one. "Are you guys crazy?" she had to ask.

"Yep," Mya said, "crazy and loving life." She walked over to Charly, then tried to hook her arm through hers. "Come on. It's time you enjoy life, too. You're here doing so much, but you're not having fun," she whined like a spoiled child. "If you're gonna hang out with us, hang out." She smiled wider, then reached into her pocket and shook something that rattled. "We've got candy!" she sang.

Charly stepped back. "I need to straighten myself up."

Rory nodded. "Yeah . . . I did a pretty decent job on your do. My fault. Handle that, sister girl, then meet us in the other room. The one with the peephole. And make sure you come too, and don't worry about a ride home. We got you, and the car isn't stolen. Promise." She looked at Charly with an apologetic face.

17

Something told her it wasn't going to be hard to figure out why Mya and Rory were acting the way they were, but it was going to be interesting, Charly thought. Rory's lazy tongue that made her slur and Mya's fit of unreasonable laughter had alerted her to trouble, and told her something was out of the ordinary. Predicaments she, herself, would avoid at all costs. She was here to fix a problem, not become part and parcel to one. She washed her hands, fixed her hair, straightened her clothes, then made her way out of the Squatters room. Liam was just across the pub, chatting with someone, and she waved her arms to get his attention while she walked over to him.

"Excuse us," Charly said to whomever. "We have a slight show emergency," she added as an afterthought, not wanting them to think she was rude.

"What happened to your face, love?" he asked, touching her softly by her ear, then turning her cheek so he could inspect her.

Charly put her hand where his had been, and felt a slight sting. She hadn't noticed the scratch in the bathroom, and hoped it wasn't as bad as it felt. She shrugged. "Listen, we have to go over there," she said, pointing to the room where Mya and Rory were.

"Cool. What's in there?"

"Trouble and solutions, hopefully," she said, then began to walk.

Liam stopped her. "What do you mean?"

"My answers about Mya. That's what's in there. I just know it. I just ran into her and Rory, and Rory was slurring and Mya was giddy. It was weird," she explained.

"Whoa. Whoa. Rory? You didn't say anything about Rory just a second ago. That changes things," he added. "So that's where the scratch came from. I knew you were hiding something. You not seeming to care about being scratched was a dead giveaway." He looked her in the eyes. "Did you lay a hand on Rory, Charly?"

Charly shook her head adamantly. "No," she told the truth. She hadn't put a hand on Rory, she'd put two. "Let's go, Liam. I need you for this one."

He nodded, then led the way to the room, pushing on the door that swung both ways.

Teenagers were everywhere. Some were posted against walls, others surrounded an iron table, and a few were on the floor staring up at the ceiling as if a box office smash were showing above them. All were either acting like zombies, drunks, or clowns, and there seemed not to be a single one who was unaffected by something. "See?"

Charly said. "See what I mean? I told you they were acting weird."

"Charly! Liam! Over here," Mya's voice called, loud
and strong, then she burst into a fit of laughter for no apparent reason. She was standing next to the table, waving
them over.

"Oh, I see you finally made it in," the guy she'd met at
the door before she went to the rest room said. "I saved
you some." He reached in his pocket, then began to pull
his hand out.

Liam reached out and stopped the guy before he could
pull out whatever from his pocket. "We're good. Thanks,"
he said, then began pulling on Charly. "I've heard about
these get-togethers. It all makes sense now—everything.
Let's go." He had her back through the swinging door
and into the pub area in seconds, but not before she saw
someone reach into the bowl, then pop something in
their mouth.

"What's this? What do you mean? What all makes
sense now? And did you see that?" she asked Liam, making her way back over to the door, and pressing her face
against the peephole, careful not to push it open. "Is that
a candy bowl?"

Liam pulled her away. "Yeah, it's candy all right.
Skittles."

Skittles. She was so tired of Skittles. It was like everywhere she looked, someone or something kept leading
her mind back to the candy. "What's up with that?" She
walked over to a table, pulled out a tall chair, then climbed
up on it. She drummed her fingers on the tabletop.

Liam joined her. "It's called a Skittles party. It's where

everyone takes their parents' medication stash, combines the loot, then they take turns picking one out. They call it Skittles because of the rainbow of colors the meds come in and not knowing what they're gonna get. It's a random selection, really, and they don't know or, possibly, even care how it'll affect them." He made a face, then began to stand. "Let's go. We can't stay around here."

Charly's jaw was on the floor. She'd suspected something was wrong, but never would've guessed prescription medication was involved. "Sit down, Liam. I'm afraid we can't leave. Rory and Mya are driving, and we can't let them do that. They're high."

Liam got up from his seat. "You can wait around here if you want, but I'm out. They're not my responsibility, and our insurance doesn't cover us for stuff like this." He eyed her. "And what if the cops come? You wanna go to jail again? This is illegal."

Charly was up on her feet before he got the last word out. She'd done jail once, she wasn't up for it again. "Got'cha. Can we just wait outside in the car?" she asked. As much as she really didn't care for Mya, and really wasn't crazy about Rory either, she wouldn't allow them to drive.

Liam was adamant, pulling out the keys to the rental car. "Not me, Charly. I'm not waiting for them to finish getting high."

He had a point, and she knew it. Mya and Rory weren't her responsibility either, but she couldn't just leave them, could she? No, she couldn't. It was clear that she'd have to get to Mya to get to Nia, and leaving Mya stranded wasn't a good way to do it. "I'll go get them. At least I'll try," she said, making her way across the pub and back to the room door with Liam on her heels.

She pushed on the door, but it wouldn't budge. She tried again, and almost lost her footing. As soon as she removed her palms, it swung toward her face, and she jumped back. "Hey," Trent greeted her. "What are you doing?" His question was filled with disappointment. He looked at Liam, then threw back his head in a what's-up fashion. "I told her to stay away," he explained.

Charly's brows rose. "I can say the same for you. Right?" she deadpanned, putting her hand on her hip. "Anyway, I was going in to get Mya and Rory so we can drive them home."

Trent shook his head. "Remember you heard me say 'wrong brother'?" Charly nodded. "Well, change the sex. Now it's wrong sister. Mya's not leaving, not with you. You may have some luck with Rory, but you're gonna have to go in and carry her out." He stuck his hands in his pockets.

Charly crossed her arms. She didn't like being dismissed so quickly. "How do you know so much?"

Trent shrugged, and a look of defeat moved across his face. "Because I'm ready to go, and I just tried to get her to leave. She won't. She won't give me the keys either, but promised to let one of my brothers drive." He kicked at the floor. "And that's really messed up. I'm the only reason they got the car, and they promised me they wouldn't—that they couldn't—because you two would be here. It was a total setup."

Liam nodded knowingly, then patted Trent on the back. "You're good. After all the help you've been giving me in the backyard, you know I wouldn't leave you stranded. You can ride with us."

Charly nodded. "Definitely," she added, feeling better. She may not have been able to pick Mya's brain about why she and Nia were clashing, but she knew Trent had answers. "So, tell me again, Trent. Why are you the only reason they got the car?" she asked as they walked out of the Juice Pub. If she didn't get anything else accomplished tonight, she'd get Trent to talk.

Trent stuck his hands in his pockets, then shrugged. "It's not really talked about anymore. It was a long time ago. No biggie," he said, following them out of the side gate to the car.

Charly shot Liam a look, and he raised his brows and frowned, then he winked as if saying "Get him, Charly." "Well, if you say so," she replied, making her way to the car. She walked quickly, making the gravel roll under her feet and dust form in the air. She looked down. "Pigpen," she said, laughing.

Liam and Trent threw her an odd glance. "Huh?" they said.

Charly shuffled her feet, making dust rise over and over. She had to get Trent to lighten up because he definitely wasn't going to spill in his current mood. He was too guarded. "Pigpen. You know, like the Charlie Brown character. C'mon, don't tell me you guys don't know about Charlie Brown and Pigpen." Trent nodded slightly, and the corners of his mouth stretched. "Don't tell me I'm the only one who had to watch the holiday specials with my mom." She looked at them both. She was pretty sure Liam had no idea what she was talking about, but she knew she had Trent's attention. The expression on his face told her so. He was just being cool about it. "You guys suck," she said, then made her way to the passenger side of the car. She stood by the door, refusing to budge, knowing if she reached for the handle, Liam would have a fit. He took the gentleman thing to heart.

Trent stopped next to her and looked at her. His face told her he didn't understand why she was just standing there. "You okay?" he asked.

Liam ran around the car, then opened the door for her. "You blokes here," he said to Trent, shaking his head. "Women aren't supposed to open doors, mate. Not if a man is around." He schooled him, then walked around to the driver's side of the car.

Trent nodded, taking it all in. "My bad. Girls around here are . . . well, girls. They don't demand that kind of respect." He opened the back door, then got into the car.

"Command," Charly corrected. "Girls demand, women command respect." She laughed, sliding into the front seat. "Even young women like me." She closed the door, then turned around in her seat, resting her arm on the headrest. "I demand a lot, but because I work hard and stay on point—keeping my word, looking out for people, and, thankfully, keeping my grades up—my character kind of commands a certain type of respect." She winked at him. She was baiting him, and hoped he'd bite. "You get it. Just like you look out for your friends. I'm sure that comes with some perks. It should." She turned around, then strapped the seat belt across her torso and lap.

Liam put his phone in the arm console, started the car, then revved the engine a little. "You want the top down?" he asked Charly.

Charly shook her head, then pointed to Liam's foot, then waved her hand, telling him to lay off the engine. She needed quiet. "No, I would love it, but I don't need any distractions. I can't zone out looking at the scenery," she said after he stopped pressing on the accelerator. "I have to work out how to pull this off. I'm running behind," she said as loud as she could so Trent could hear. She widened her eyes, looking intently at Liam, then said under her breath, "Star power. Remember?"

Liam nodded then grinned. "Now you got it." He pulled off. "Well, cash in some of your perks. As much as you help other people, it shouldn't be a problem."

Trent sat up, then leaned forward as much the seat belt would allow. "What are all these perks you two keep talking about?"

Charly smiled at him, nodding. He was playing right into her hand just as she had planned, but it would be worth it for all involved. No matter what, she promised herself, she was ready to bargain. He'd wanted to help Liam with the set, so that meant he'd be even more willing to help her with her portion of the show. No, he wasn't one of the extra hands who'd offered their services for a little publicity. She looked back at him and just stared, knowing the silence would just turn up his curiosity. Plus, she needed to size him up. If she got her way, she'd have to make him over too so he'd be camera-ready, and that meant making him a heartthrob. With one glance, his being an easy fix was apparent. He had features she could definitely work with, and was definitely a bonus for the special summer makeover show. He was a local and, on top of that, a teen whom Nia liked, so why not use him? She was sure she would be able to negotiate him some camera time, and knew he wanted it. She nodded. Yes, she'd spread her wings and turn into the angel who'd change his life while she changed others'. The town would shine when she was finished with it. Nia, Trent, the cast and crew, the locals and the town. That's one of the things star power was for—getting to the top—and that's just what she planned to do. "Perks. You know, like karma. When you do good things for people, good things come back to you. You know, like Mya and Rory and your brothers and whoever else using you so they could go to the pub."

"Used? I never thought about it like that. But now that you've said it, that's exactly what they did. Just like they did to Nia." He had finally spilled, and Charly knew it was only the beginning.

18

Trent sat in the back, taking it all in. Charly and Liam played up the show, said how fun it was to watch themselves on television, and explained how life changing it was. Every time the conversation between them started to dwindle, she'd switch topics. She had to make Trent want a piece of the limelight enough to ask for it, otherwise she wouldn't have enough bargaining power, she told herself.

Liam hung a left, then a right, and sped down the road. It was dark out, nothing but the moon and stars lighting their way. "I know you don't want to hear this, Charly," he said, winking. "But since I've been on television, my female pull has quadrupled. You should know," he said, catching himself because Trent was a fan, and the unspoken rule of the show was the world was supposed to wonder if Charly and Liam were really an item. Their possibly being together, combined with all the on-camera flirting only brought up the ratings. "As many as you've had to fight off." He laughed.

Charly jokingly punched him in the arm. "Very funny. Ha ha. I thought you were going to let me drive," she said, pleading with her eyes.

Liam crinkled his brow and rotated his head left and right so hard, Charly was sure it was going to unscrew and fall off. "Didn't you just get out of jail for driving?"

She glared at him. "You promised, and I *need* to. Really, really need to . . . for the show. Um. Um . . ." She grasped for a believable lie. "At some point, I have to drive to the stores, so they want me to practice," she said, knowing it was an awful tale, but how was Trent to know? He didn't work in the entertainment business.

Liam exhaled, then reluctantly pulled over. "I don't know, Charly . . ." he said, putting the car in park.

"It'll be fine, Liam. Trust me. I didn't go to jail because I can't drive. I went to jail because of Rory using me," she said, emphasizing *using* for Trent's sake. She needed him to feel like he'd been used so he could fess up.

"Rory?" he said from behind, making a tsking noise. "Doesn't surprise me."

Charly didn't respond as she climbed over the arm console and sat on the driver's side when Liam got out. She adjusted the mirrors, then moved the seat forward until her feet touched the pedals. "Strap in," she said to Liam, then put the car in DRIVE and pulled off. "So, yeah, Trent. Rory? She had me drive for her and I got locked up. I can't believe she used me like that. I'm surprised you didn't hear."

"Oh, I heard. Just not all of it, apparently," he said,

then pointed his finger. "When you get to the stop sign, turn left." He was quiet for a second. "Ya know, Charly, that's really messed up that she played you like that."

Charly nodded, then tapped her foot on the brake, gently and quickly, making the car jerk. "What's wrong?" she asked no one, then pressed the accelerator again causing the convertible to coast smoothly. "Um. Nothing, I guess," she said, then sped to the stop sign, looked both ways, then turned left as Trent had instructed.

Liam looked over at her, then leaned his upper body over the arm console and eyed the dashboard. He moved back into his seat. "That's strange. There's no warning lights on, and it wasn't jerking earlier."

Charly nodded. "Well, that's good to know," she said, sneaking and tapping the brakes again as she spoke. The car jerked and bounced under the press of her foot, then stopped when she shoed the brake to the floor. She banged the dashboard. "C'mon, you can't be serious!" She put it in PARK.

Liam looked at the console again, shaking his head. "I don't get it." He rubbed his head in irritation. "This can't be good. How far are we from your house, Trent? Or civilization? Whichever comes first is good."

Trent sat up, looking around. "We're on Potters," he said, like that meant anything to anyone beside himself. "So that means we're far away from everything." He started patting his pockets. "It's no biggie though. We have a mechanic in another town. He'll come get us," he assured, still rubbing his hands on the outside of his jeans pockets, then his shirt. "Man. I must've left my phone, and I don't know his number. And he's bootlegged too—meaning he has no registered business number, so calling information or Googling it won't help."

Before Liam could maneuver his arm around the console to open it from Charly's side where the button was located, Charly beat him to it, and took out his phone. She gave his screen a quick look, then shook her head in disgust. "I can't believe there's no reception in this town!" she yelled as if she were out of her mind, throwing Liam and Trent for a loop. She reached into her pocket, then took out her cell, and glanced at it. "Absolutely none! There is absolutely no reception on my phone or yours. And we're in the middle of nowhere!" she snapped again, holding both phones in one hand, and reaching for her bag with the other. Liam looked scared, and reached onto the floor. He retrieved her bag, and handed it to her. "We don't have *any* bars," she lied, stuffing both Liam's phone and hers into her purse.

An uncomfortable look masked Liam's face. He cleared his throat, then shook his head. "Dead? Really? Both of them?" His expression said he wanted to question her, but he didn't. Instead, he reached toward Charly. "Can you pass me my phone?"

Charly went selectively deaf, then banged the steering wheel. "Liam, what are we going to do?" She sounded as if she were going to cry. She turned and looked at Trent. "Well? Someone say something. Trent? C'mon. It's because of your friends not being your real friends that we're out here. If they weren't using you, we wouldn't have had to take you home. That's why we're here, right?

So, you have to come up with something!" She knew she was making him feel bad, but she needed Trent to get angry. His face was a mask of defeat.

Trent shrugged, then threw up his hands.

Charly tsked, then shook her head. "I'm sorry, Trent. I just hate to see people taken advantage of. Especially people like you and Nia," she said, trying to make him spill about how Nia had been used. "We really don't mind taking you home." She eased the keys out of the ignition, then opened the driver's door.

"Where are you going?" Liam asked.

Charly dug in her purse, then pulled out a phone. "I have Rory's number locked in. I just want to walk to see if I can get reception. You can stay there or come with." She paused, pressing her lips together. "Well, maybe not. I kind of have to tinkle, too. Plus, I'm only going to walk a few feet. I'll be in your view the whole time, except when I take my behind-the-bushes break," she assured, then made her way down the road where they could still see her, but not hear her.

She could see Liam and Trent talking, and hoped Liam was pulling information out of him. She held her phone up in the air as if she were really looking for reception, but she wasn't. Her phone had never lost it, but she needed Trent to think so. She felt bad for not letting Liam in on her charade, but she didn't have time to preplan, and Trent was too close for her to divulge without being overheard. "I got some," she yelled, waving her arm. She pretended to dial, then pressed the phone to her ear. She was playing dirty, and she knew she should've felt bad about it, but she didn't. Someone was toying with her too, according to the Skittles wrapper, and she believed it. Her not being able to get to Nia like she needed to and all the other sideline drama didn't allow for her to play fair. She had a mission to accomplish, and nothing was going to stop her. "Oh, no!" Charly yelled, then stomped back toward the car. "Can you believe this?" she asked. "Those . . . those . . . I can't even call them what I want to call them. I told them we were stuck on Potters. I think that's what you said—right, Trent?" He nodded. "Well, they said that's too bad. They're not done partying, so we're on our own."

Trent huffed, and anger engulfed him. Charly didn't think she'd ever seen someone who looked so angry, never mind actually felt that way. "Who?" he barked. "Who said we were on our own?"

Charly paused, summoning her inner actress. She'd been doing reality television for so long, her acting skills had gone unpracticed. She put her hand to her chest, reared back her head, then sneered, exposing all her teeth. Like a wicked witch, she laughed eerily, then tailored it until it sounded of disgust. "I called Rory's phone, but Mya answered."

Trent now stepped completely out of his character. He wasn't just angry, he was beyond infuriated. He rubbed his chin with his hand, then bit his lip. Finally, he broke, and cursed loud and rapidly, saying words and phrases Charly had never heard before. He nodded. "Okay. It's like that. A'ight," he said, losing all of his boy-next-door charm. "And after they used us!" He looked at Liam, then turned to Charly. "So you wanna know what went down between Mya and Nia?"

19

Her upper body was housed between the car hood and the engine. Liam held up the cell phone, trying to give her light while she tinkered with wires, the oil cap and, finally, some other part she couldn't have identified if her life depended on it.

"After that, Mya refused to let Nia drive. The next thing you know, because of Mya's stupidity, her and Nia were wrapped around a tree. The car had literally bent in a semicircle. That's where Nia got that scar from." Trent kicked at a rock. He was venting, letting everything out, and he didn't seem to want to stop. He'd told them the whole story and, it was obvious Mya's partying and being under the influence was normal behavior for her.

"So why was Nia there again?" Charly asked. "Liam, go try to start the car." She reached in her pocket, then threw Liam the keys. She looked over her shoulder at a pacing Trent, waiting for him to answer.

Trent stopped and held Charly with his stare. "Nia went because she *had* to go, and she didn't want to. I remember that like it was yesterday because I'm the one who told her not to go . . . I'm also the one who tried to stop her from getting in the car." He looked in the sky as if remembering. "She'd even offered to drop off Mya at the party, but their parents, back then, wouldn't dare go for that. Nia and Mya were like Noah's ark passengers—in twos. If one twin went, the other had to. So each weekend they took turns deciding where to go. That night, it was Mya's turn, and Nia wasn't pleased with the choice."

The engine purred, making Liam and Trent come to life. Charly swiped the grime off her hands like she'd really done something, then smiled. She wasn't smiling because the car started, she was grinning because she'd gotten everything she needed from Trent. "Come on," Liam urged them from the driver's seat.

"I never understood why they had to share a car because their dad has plenty of chop," he said, referring to how much money Nia and Mya's father had, then got in the car. "Liam, if you keep heading straight for about three miles, then take a right, we'll be there."

As soon as Trent got out of the car, Charly sat in silence. Neither she nor Liam spoke for what seemed like eternity because she was so tired. But she needed the quiet to reflect and plan. After miles, the dark streets were finally lit. Charly sighed, glad that they'd finally entered civilization, and were now passing office buildings. She turned and looked at Liam, hoping he could shed some light on the matter. She'd heard everything Trent said, but the story was fragmented. In over an hour, all she'd learned was that what she was working with wasn't pretty. The sisters were rivals because of Mya, and her losing her driving privileges made sense to Charly, but what she couldn't understand was why Mya disliked Nia so much. Nia was the victim, not the other way around.

"Still makes no sense, huh?" Liam asked, finally turning onto the street the hotel was on. "Just like the car stalling on us back there. I just don't get it."

Charly's frown was guilty. Her brows were raised, eyes were saucers, and her lips were poked out. "Sorry . . ." she said, shrugging.

"What? What did you do, Charly St. James?" Liam asked. He didn't look angry, he looked lost, and she loved it.

"The car never stalled, and the phones always had reception. That was all me. I did what I had to do to get what I wanted . . . from Trent," she admitted. "But I'm going to hook him up. See what I can find for him to do on the set. Star power."

To her surprise, Liam nodded. His expression said he was impressed. "Remind me to buy you dinner." His lips spread into a smile. He reached over, then grabbed her hand and put it to his mouth. Charly thought she was going to die when his soft lips kissed it. "That was a professional player move, Charly. I'm impressed. You got what you wanted from Trent, but the rest still doesn't add up. Does it?"

Charly shook her head. She didn't have an answer, and

didn't feel like figuring it out. It would take time to get to the truth, and Nia too. Charly looked at her watch, and saw that it was too late to pop over there now, but she certainly wanted to. She needed to look Nia in the face, appeal to her, twist her arm or whatever it took to get the information she needed. Trent had given her the basics, but didn't understand why Nia was the way she was or why Mya was the head bee in the house. She tsked. For some reason she knew Nia wouldn't talk, but then again, Nia might've been unaware of her sister's dislike herself, Charly reasoned. The shift of power was directed at Mya, who was clearly the stronger of the two.

The car pulled to a stop in the front of the hotel. "Go ahead, love. I'll park and meet you upstairs."

Charly looked at Liam and shook her head. "I'm good. I'll go with you. It's not like my feet are hurting or anything." Liam reached over and touched her face. "Ouch!" Charly replied.

"It's swelling. I'm sure the front desk has an emergency kit," he said, mashing his foot on the parking brake.

Charly had her purse in her hand and was out of the car in seconds. "Done. See you in a few." Her face swelling was all she needed to hear to make her hurry. She was pushing through the rotating door, and headed to the counter when she caught sight of Heaven. "Oh, no."

Heaven looked at her, then did a double take. "Charly!" she said, her usual dead-sounding voice filled with life. "I didn't expect to see you so soon."

Charly looked at Heaven, sure she'd fallen and bumped

her head, forgetting how morbid she usually was. She was definitely out of character. Charly guessed it was going around. First Trent, and now Heaven. "Uh . . . hi. I guess," Charly said, looking around.

Heaven jerked back in shock, then put her hand over her heart as if she were having a heart attack. She smiled, and Charly was sure she was going to pass out. She didn't think Heaven knew how to grin. "Oh, my . . . what happened?" Heaven asked, feigning surprise. "I've never seen you at a loss for words."

Charly just wide-eyed her, wondering who this girl was in front of her. Heaven hadn't been at the party, so she couldn't accuse her of being on drugs. She crinkled her brow, then leaned on the counter. "Do you have any Band-Aids and antiseptic?"

Heaven burst out laughing. "For you, Charly St. James, we have anything. *Anything.*" She went into a room situated off to the side, then reappeared in seconds. In her hand was a first-aid kit. "Here," she said. "You need any help?"

Charly just stared at her.

Heaven snapped her fingers in Charly's face. "Wake up, Charly. You must be tired because I know you're not on anything. You're no pill popper. I already got a call to confirm." She nodded. "Good for you. And good for you for beating down Rory too. I had you all wrong. You and Liam." She pressed her lips together. "I apologize for that, and I should know better too. People are always judging me before they know me, and I hate that. So if there's anything I can do for you, name it. I owe you at least that much."

Liam walked through the door, looking tired. He was dragging his feet and rolling his suitcases behind him, which told Charly he must've been coming back to her room because, the last time she'd heard, the hotel was booked.

Charly leaned on the counter. "Is there any way you could find Liam a room? Did anyone check out?" She paused. "We'll be willing to pay, of course. We're not into taking the hotel's money or advantage of you being so nice. I just need him to get some rest, and him sleeping here in the lobby won't do." *Because there's no way he's crashing in my room again—not with all this attraction,* she wanted to say, but opted not to.

Heaven started punching the keyboard keys. She pressed her lips together, really concentrating. "Well . . . we did have a no-show yesterday. They're paid up until the day after tomorrow, and they still haven't checked in." She shrugged. "You do understand it doesn't mean they won't show up tonight? So I can't guarantee he won't be interrupted, but I can guarantee he'll at least have a place to lay his head. For now."

Charly nodded, then rubbed Liam's arm, who had finally made it to her side. "Cool. I thank you so much. If there's anything I can do for you, Heaven," she said, waiting for Heaven to finish making the card key for Liam's sleeping quarters.

The machine clicked twice, then spit out the hotel key. Heaven took it, stuck it in a minifolder, then handed it to Liam. "For you," she said with a smile on her face. Liam returned the grin, and looked as surprised as Charly had when Heaven first greeted her with niceness. "And you," Heaven said to Charly. "There is something you can do for me; you can get to the mayor. He has all the answers you want. Politicians aren't just liars, they're great hiders."

20

Her bag was over her shoulder and her attitude was to the heavens, but there was nothing angelic about it. Charly marched up the back staircase, headed toward Nia's room. She wanted answers, and would get them. Today. Her knuckles were rapping on Nia's door before she knew it, but she didn't answer. Charly pressed her ear to the wood and listened. There was movement inside the room. It was faint, but she heard it. She balled her fist, then banged on the door like she was equipped with a badge and a warrant. She stepped back, crossed her arms, then tapped her foot.

"Oh, hey, Charly," Mya's voice called out from the staircase.

Charly turned, watching Mya step onto the landing. She was smiling like everything was everything. Charly forced herself to return the politeness Mya had offered her. It wasn't an easy thing to do, especially now that she considered Mya a druggie. "Hey back," she said, turning on her heels. She figured if she couldn't get to the sister she'd come to see, as long as she got to one of them, it was still progress. "What are you getting ready to do?"

Mya threw up her hands in the air, then dropped them to her sides. "I don't have anything planned. What's up?" She now stood at her bedroom door with her hand on the knob.

"Yes, you do. You have a lot to do," Charly said, her voice a combination of forced sweetness laced with a demanding tone. "Let's shoot over to the city so we can get some shopping done."

Mya's face brightened, telling Charly that Charly was now speaking her language. "Cool. Let me grab my purse and phone, and I'll be ready." She paused. "You're driving, right?"

Charly laughed low and knowing. "Because you can't, right?" She smirked. "No worries. I had the studio send a car here this morning. It's outside. Liam has to work, so he can't run me around. I'll meet you out front."

Mya had talked the entire ride, and Charly regretted not being able to make Liam tag along. It wasn't fair that she had to suffer Mya's being full of herself on her lonesome. She felt bad for the hired driver and worse for herself because she had to sit in the backseat of the town car with the talker of the year. For almost an hour, Mya had gone on and on about herself, making Charly want to regurgitate in her own mouth. She was sure that tasting her own vomit was more appealing than listening to Mya and her never-ending conversation about nothing. The girl had spoken about not one thing of interest and, after ten minutes Charly questioned if she and Nia were really twins. After twenty, she wondered if they were related at all. Charly looked at her, waiting for her to collapse because she was sure Mya was going to deflate and puddle on the seat. She had no substance, so she was an empty shell. Charly blinked slowly, knowing she had to be mistaken. There was no way in the world Mya could be as dense as she presented herself to be, not after she and Nia were both excellent students before Mya's departure from herself to obviously being like the in crowd.

"Mya," Charly said, interrupting her as she was in the middle of talking about a pair of red-bottom shoes she thought she needed. "I need your opinion on something." Mya looked up, giving Charly her attention. "How do you do it?" Charly asked, baiting her. She needed to see which side, strong or weak, would appeal to Mya.

"Do what?" She perked up, apparently liking to be needed.

"You know, how do you handle always having to be the strongest? The leader and the one everyone looks to? I have a younger sister, and it's hard for me. Everything rests in my lap, as my dad would say." Charly sounded sincere, but she wasn't. Her younger sister meant the world to her, and there was nothing she wouldn't do for her.

Mya paused, then picked up her phone and started checking her text messages. Charly had obviously lost her attention. Mya shrugged. "I dunno what to tell you because I couldn't care less. I don't do weakness, Charly. If my sister wants to lie on the floor like a doormat, then that's her choice. I don't let her problems become mine and vice versa," she said, never looking up. Her words were void of any feeling, and Charly knew she'd have to handle her differently to get through to her. She resumed talking about red-bottom shoes.

The driver pulled the car alongside the curb, parked, and got out to open their door. Charly reached over and put her hand over Mya's phone. Gently, she pushed it down toward her lap, and it took everything in her to be so kind. What she really wanted to do was slap it out of her hands for being so rude. "I wasn't done talking, so don't igg me when I talk." Her voice was edgy as she instructed Mya on not ignoring her. "Please," she forced herself to say.

Mya's blank expression said she was clueless, but a flicker of something was behind her eyes that gave Charly hope that she wasn't. "Oh, I didn't know. What's up?"

Charly heard a click, then felt wind on her back when the driver opened the door. She rotated her body and flashed him a smile, then thanked him, grabbing her purse and stepping out of the car. She looked around at the shoppers while waiting for Mya to exit the back, which was taking a lot longer than expected. The driver stood at the door, waiting patiently for Mya who, Charly discovered after she bent forward and glanced inside the town car, was refreshing her pressed powder and lip gloss. Her patience had died, and her tolerance was waning. She cleared her throat, then tried to calm herself. She knew she couldn't get on Mya's good side if she handled her the way she wanted. In order to get Mya to play into her hand, she'd first have to pretend to play into Mya's. She stood straight, breathed deeply, and summoned her inner actress again. *I can do this,* she assured herself. *I can dumb down. That's all it's going to take,* she tried to convince herself as she squared her shoulders and prepared for what she was sure was going to be the longest shopping trip of her life.

Mya finally made her appearance, one motion at a time, like she was a celebrity on the red carpet. Charly watched the deliberate exit unfold in front of her in three steps. First, Mya stretched her leg out of the car, setting her foot on the ground just so. Her hand extended to the driver next, and she placed her palm on top of his like she was a queen and he was there to kiss her ring. Carefully, like she was fragile and would break, she gripped his, then got out ever so slowly, making Charly exhale in appreciation of the show being over. Now standing tall, Mya stopped and paused, slipped on a pair of sunglasses, then shook her hair like she was being taped for a shampoo commercial.

"Ugh," Charly said, disgusted. She took a few steps, then reached over and grabbed Mya's arm, pulling it. "Thank you, and sorry," she said to the driver, who smiled and tried to conceal his distaste for Mya's dramatics. "No cameras, Mya," Charly said, walking toward the entrance of a ritzy mall that housed high-end shops.

Mya smiled, adjusting her sunglasses and keeping in step with Charly. "What do you mean?"

Frustrated, Charly stopped, then stepped in Mya's path to block her. "Not today, Mya. Today, you get to be yourself. You don't have to perform for me. I *know* who you are. Who you *really* are. So no need for the antics."

Mya's perfectly arched brows lost their perfection

when she crinkled them. "What do you mean by *antics,* Charly? What are you implying? Because it sounds to me like you're accusing me of being other than who I am. You don't know me, Charly. So don't pretend to." Her arms were crossed and her I'm-too-pretty-to-be-myself façade had come tumbling down, replaced by an attitude of one who was certain about her true self, not some feigned popular air.

Charly clenched her teeth to prevent from smiling. She knew there was depth somewhere inside of Mya, and she'd discovered it, thanks to Mya's annoying her. Charly began to walk, throwing her head in the air. She could give Mya exactly what Mya gave everyone else—showmanship with the worst sportsmanship possible. Now that she'd resurrected the true Mya, it was time for her to tame her. To show her what it felt like to be treated small and insignificant, what she'd apparently been doing a lot to her sister. Charly looked over her shoulder at Mya, then turned her head, making her longer tendrils float in the wind. Borrowing a tactic from Mya, she reached into her purse, took out her sunglasses, then slid them on her face. Not once did she reply to Mya, who kept clearing her throat as if reminding Charly that she hadn't answered her. Charly stopped in front of the mall entrance door, and stepped to the side. She would show Mya one step at a time who was really the star. Mya had local celebrity status, Charly was now global.

"Really? So you have nothing to say for yourself?" Mya said, opening the door and getting ready to walk through it, but Charly beat her to it.

"Thanks," Charly said, as if Mya had purposely held

open the door for her, which, in her opinion, was being too nice, but someone had to teach the girl some manners. Mya hadn't even thanked their driver.

Mya grimaced, then stomped her foot like a child. "Charly? What's your problem?" she asked, standing in the doorway.

Charly turned and looked at her. She removed her sunglasses and stared at her, never batting a lash. "You're my problem, Mya. My problem and everyone else's, it seems." She laughed and shook her head. "Funny how you've tricked everyone else. Well, at least you thought so." She shrugged. "But the funny thing about being a star—a real one, and not one who pretends to be just to hurt other people, namely your sister, Nia, is that when you're a real star you get something called star power. In my case, that consists of a team of researchers who get paid to get the background information on the families we select." She blinked slowly, then tilted her head and smiled. "In doing a check for the show, a lot of dirt was uncovered. Secrets—juicy life-changing secrets about your family— came to light. And, I'm disappointed really. What you did to your sister that night you crashed the car . . ." She shook her head. "It's a shame. How could you be so heartless? Now we're stuck. You guys had buried your dirt so deep it's just starting to reveal itself, and we don't know how to proceed. The show's been approved so we have to do it, but who knows," she said, shrugging. "We may just have to cancel it and, possibly, reveal why: the mayor's daughter is a druggie, and Daddy Dearest covers up for her, so the other sister has to suffer." She stretched her eyes. "And that would be even more of a shame than how you treat Nia, because your dad has reelections coming up soon, right?" Charly finished, then turned around. She'd just cast her rod to bait and hook the fish, and knew Mya was going to bite, so there was no use in standing around. She knew Mya would spill before they finished shopping.

21

Mya's hand was on Charly's shoulder before she made it to the escalator. "You're not going to say anything about my family." A demand, not a question.

Charly turned and looked at Mya's hand, then up to her eyes. "Catch yourself or catch a beat down, Mya," she warned, then shook Mya's hand off her. "I'm not Nia, and you put not an ounce of fear in my heart or a pause in my thinking. I'll curl you around one of these poles in here. I have no respect for you," Charly admitted. If Liam were there, he'd chastise her like she was a child, but he wasn't there and she wasn't being immature. She was just doing what she had to to get what she wanted. That included saving Nia and, now, Mya too, if only from herself and prescription meds. Adrenaline raced through Charly's veins. Being touched wasn't something she liked. Yes, she knew she was pushing Mya, but she had to. Getting under Mya's skin was the only way she was going to get through Nia's barrier, but first she had to find out why it was there. Mya had the answer, and Charly knew it.

Mya nodded, but not in agreement. Her head moving was a sign of her strength, it was more like an I-dare-you nod than one of fear. "You don't have to respect me, Charly. However, you're not going to disrespect me either. Not to my face."

Charly stepped up. "Oh no?" She shook her head. "Because you're going to do what? Stop me?"

Mya stood her ground. "No, because you don't know who I am—you don't know my sister either. You think she's all innocent? That she's the victim? Nia's the problem, not the solution!" Mya raised her voice.

"I know that your dad's career is on the line if you don't tell me the truth." Charly felt her principles fall with each bullying tactic she used, but she had to fight fire with something of a supernova power. Regular heat wasn't enough. Mya was stronger than she'd thought.

Mya's eyes began to water, and Charly didn't know if she was tearing because she was angry or hurt. Whatever the reason behind the emotion, Charly appreciated it because it meant she'd struck something. Finally, she began to breathe, feeling progress approaching. "There's a café on the other side of the mall. Let's go there," Mya said, pointing.

A bottle of Perrier sat on the table in front of Charly, alongside a toasted bagel. Charly crossed her legs, sitting sideways in her chair. She bounced her foot, watching Mya. She'd sat in silence for minutes, using a French fry to move around the buffalo shrimp on her plate, looking like she had no intention of eating. Charly was waiting for her to speak, but she acted like her lips were as glued to the plate as her fingers were to the food. "So you're not going to eat at all?" Charly asked.

Mya looked up and locked eyes with her. Her expression was one of a guilty child who'd been caught red-handed doing something they'd been told not to do. "What do you want me to say? You want me to hang my family?" She sucked her teeth. "That's not going to happen."

Charly's breath caught in her throat. Here she was pushing Mya for the truth, and she'd come across all wrong. She wasn't trying to hurt her or her family, but could now see why she'd take it that way. "I'm not trying to get you to turn against your family, Mya. You got it all wrong. I'm just trying to discuss Nia." She leaned over the table, looking into Mya's eyes, pleading with her.

Tears tracked down Mya's face. "Yes, that's what you said, Charly. And who gives an eff about Nia? I don't. Why should I? It's always Nia *this*, Nia *that*. Nia's going to get a scholarship and she's barely fifteen years old," Mya huffed. "Nia's the smartest twin. I thought identical twins are supposed to be identical?" she blurted at top speed, moving her hand like a mouth opening and closing as if she had a puppet on it. She looked at Charly colder than anyone ever had. "You can talk about my sister all you want. I don't care about that. I'm used to it, especially since the accident. She wallows in pity and plays on people's emotions because of it. But I won't hand my father to you. He's a good guy, and he's never done anything wrong to anyone. Plus, he's *all* I got." She reached in her purse, then took out her shades, and slid them on her face. She picked up her glass, took a sip, and looked off to the side at shoppers.

Charly lost her breath. She sat back in her seat, taking in what Mya had just admitted. The rivalry between the twins was now obvious, at least from Mya's perspective, and that Charly could understand. But Mya's stating that her father was all she had, told Charly it was about so much more than grades. "Oh, Mya," Charly said, getting out of her seat. She reached into her purse, took out enough cash to cover the food bill and tip, then tossed it on the table. She walked to the other side of the bistro table, and extended her hand to Mya. Her gesture surprised them both, and Charly realized that she'd grown a lot because she recognized she was wrong, and had no problem owning up to it. "We're going to have to agree to disagree. I've got my take on what I said, and you have yours. But I assure you, I was not threatening your dad or trying to get you to throw him under the bus. I know he's a good guy. Everyone does. If I came across that way to you, I apologize."

Mya slid her sunglasses down her nose, then looked up into Charly's face. Her eyes were red and her expression was stoic. "You mean it?"

Charly nodded. "Yes, Mya, I do." She waited for Mya to take her hand, accept her apology, do something—

anything that would hint to her believing Charly was sincere.

Mya stood up, ignoring Charly's proffered hand. "Okay, but it's going to cost you." She gripped her bag close to her side, then began walking away. "And more than the meal too," she said, looking over her shoulder at Charly. "C'mon. We're here to shop for my dad, right? So let's go. On our way here, on the other side of the mall, I saw a perfect chair for his new office. That should compensate for my wounded feelings."

Charly just stood, shaking her head. She knew she had it coming, and was prepared to pay the price for making Mya cry, she just didn't think she'd literally have to cough up cash. Even though she knew Mya was going to hit her pockets hard, she had to smile. She guessed that in a very small way, they were alike. They both shone when they walked in a room and, like Mya, Charly was protective of her family. She would stand up and fight for whomever she loved, just as she would for whatever she believed in. She watched Mya walking ahead of her, and her glance moved down to her feet. Charly nodded. They both had a mean shoe game too, but Charly's was better, she told herself, running to catch up with Mya. They still hadn't discussed the night before and the Skittles party.

"Hurry, Charly! Or else I'm going to find shoes to match the chair." Mya turned to her, smiling and teasing.

Charly nodded and returned the smile. She'd tormented the girl enough, she told herself. They would just shop and talk, side by side, as equals. Mya was acting more mature, and Charly guessed it wasn't an act, but the real her.

She wasn't being over the top for attention, and didn't have to compete with Charly like she obviously felt she had to do with her sister, who was smarter. No, she could just be her. Charly only hoped that that included her being open and honest about the pill popping because Charly wouldn't be able to leave until it was addressed.

22

The blacktop was getting ready to meet her face. It was all happening so quickly, yet so slowly. Inch by inch, every miniscule detail of the driveway—cracks, ladybugs, weeds—was in her vision, growing bigger and larger as her head drew closer to the pavement that was supposed to be under her feet. And would've, had she not stumbled out of the backseat of the car, tripping over her own shoes. Charly reached out her hands to prevent her fall, but it wasn't possible. Her palms slapped the ground, stinging, but she didn't care. She laughed, loud and hard, and tears were forming in her eyes.

"I told you to watch out! But no!" Mya said, getting out of the car. She was laughing and holding her stomach with one hand, and was equipped with two shopping bags in the other.

In a push-up position, Charly pushed up her body a foot from the blacktop, and saw feet walking toward her.

She looked up higher and locked eyes with Liam, who just smiled at her. He adjusted his baseball hat, wiped his hands on his jeans, and made his way over to her. "C'mon, love. You're too pretty to be down there," he teased, complimenting her and squatting down. He put his hands under her arms and lifted her completely off the ground as if she were as light as air.

Charly was still laughing when he spun her around in a complete circle, then put her down. "Thank you," she said, wrapping her arms around him and squeezing tight. She'd only been gone from him for hours, but she missed him, his sanity and evenness. With Liam there was never a problem, and nothing he couldn't seem to handle or get through.

"What a nice surprise. You should go shopping more often." Liam embraced her, then rocked her slowly. "Seems like someone had a good time," he whispered in her ear.

"I did," she admitted, forgetting that Mya was standing nearby. For a quick second, she worried how Mya felt about Liam and her hugging, but dismissed the thought. Liam was hers, period. It didn't matter that they weren't really an item, that they hadn't made anything official. That they hadn't even had a discussion about being involved or not. It just was what it was, and he wasn't available.

"Well, I wish I could report to you that that feeling was felt across the board today," he said, tilting his head toward the house. "Your girl has had a bit of a rough day, I'm afraid." His beautiful accent made Nia's dilemma sound better than Charly knew it was. Liam's pronunciation made everything sound delicious. He looked into Charly's eyes and told her everything she needed to know without words. Something bad had happened.

Charly looked toward the house, and, sure enough, she caught sight of Nia in the upstairs window. She was certain that, like before, Nia would disappear from view, but she was wrong. Nia stood there taking in the whole scene, and she didn't look too happy about it. Charly was about to wave to her, then realized she couldn't. She was still in Liam's arms. "Um . . ." she began, looking at him.

"Um, what, love? Didn't you do excellent in your English class? You know *um* isn't a word, right?" he joked.

Charly rolled her eyes and smiled. "Do you think it's a good idea for us to be all hugged up in front of them?"

"Oh," Liam said, sounding surprised like he didn't know he had her wrapped in his arms. He released her quickly, jumping back like Charly was fire and he didn't want to get burned.

"Hi, Liam." Mya finally spoke from behind, her tone light and friendly.

Charly looked over her shoulder at the girl she'd been hanging with all day—the girl she'd learned a lot about and now liked—and hoped she wouldn't have to check Mya. It would've been bad for everything to go sour now that they'd made so much progress. Thankfully, Mya didn't display her usual overly flirtatiousness. Instead, she gave Charly a look that said do-your-thing, and smiled pleasantly.

Liam spoke back, then went over and took Mya's bags from her, then turned to Charly. "Where are your bags, love?" he asked, standing by the car. Charly pointed to the trunk. He smiled. "I knew you couldn't go shopping and come back empty-handed." He walked to the back of the car, meeting the driver, who handed him one small robin's-egg blue bag. Liam turned and looked at Charly. "*Tiffany?*" He raised his brows in approval.

Charly waved him over, waiting for him. "Mya, I'll meet you in the house. I need to get some work in, then we'll finish where we left off. Cool?" she asked, then laced her arm through Liam's when he walked over to her. "I need you to catch me up on Nia, but I need to tell you about today with Mya. This is complicated, but easy. An oxymoron, I know, but it seems everything around here is. I don't know who should go first. I got a lot to tell you," Charly said to him as low as she could. "In the pool house, though. We definitely can't speak around anyone," she began.

They walked around the side of the property on the cobblestone path. Liam looked at her. "Trent's here—"

Charly stopped in her tracks. "Already?" She shook her head, knowing it couldn't be good. When they'd dropped him off he was hotter than fish grease, he was so mad his temperature had to be bubbling.

"Rory, too," Liam said. "You need to do a lot of damage control. A whole lot." He resumed walking. "Trent and Rory got into it, and Nia overheard them. Trent, though, is a good guy. He was defending Nia, blaming "pill heads" for Nia's scar and depression. I think that only made her feel worse."

Charly's sight dropped to the ground, watching her feet as if they held the answers she knew she'd have to come up with. She hadn't expected her truth-seeking lie

to surface so soon. Really, she hadn't planned on anything coming out. Her plan was to get to the truth, fix it,
then maybe, just maybe, tell them what she'd done. The
cobblestone path gave way to the concrete patio, and
Charly looked up. The pool house was in view, and so
were Rory and Trent who, thankfully, were on the other
side of the backyard preoccupied with building materials.
Liam hustled over to the door, opening it before anyone
caught sight of Charly.

"Hurry," he rushed. "C'mon in, love. I really don't
want to have to use some of the power equipment to save
you, but I will." He winked, standing to the side so any
view of her would be blocked from the other side of the
yard.

Charly stepped inside, then moved her body to the side
of the doorway. Trent and Rory and Nia, all meeting and
clashing because of her was too much. Her heart raced
now, and her thoughts stared to twirl over and over in
her mind as she tried to find the words to defuse the situation.

Liam shut the door, then turned the lock until it
clicked. He walked over to a box, then sat on it. He patted it. "It's good. There's a minifridge in here, so it's not
going to collapse under me, love. I don't want you to
have to hurt yourself, coming to my rescue and all." He
tried to make light of the situation. "So, you want to go
first?" he asked calmly.

Charly slid down the wall, then sat with her legs folded
one over the other. She put her face in her hands. She
needed a moment to digest having to face an angry group
after she left the safety of the pool house. Running her

fingers through her hair, she exhaled, then sat up. "It's simple, really. Mya and Nia were twin everything until something that happened recently to drive a wedge between them. The only thing they didn't share was time, thanks to their parents, who probably thought they were doing the right thing." Liam raised his brows in curiosity. "It seems that Mommy and Daddy Dearest didn't want the girls to ever feel like they'd missed out on any kind of love or affection—or be treated like twins, where they'd have to share everything—so the parents divided their attention. Nia was Mommy's girl. Mya was Daddy's." She shrugged her shoulders. "This, in my opinion, makes perfect sense because each baby had constant care from a parent, and didn't have to deal with being juggled. The problem came in later. Nia excelled academically, Mya didn't."

Liam interjected. "So while Nia was receiving praise, I'm assuming from both parents, Mya felt abandoned. That's why she resents her sister." He pressed his lips together, looked up to the ceiling, then nodded. "Makes sense."

Charly shook her head. "It gets worse. Everyone praised Nia—Mommy, Daddy, the school. Pretty much the whole town after Nia was scouted heavily by universities after taking her pre-SATs two years earlier than most." She got up, then walked over to the window facing the pool, and peeked out. "So," she said, turning around. "It's a small town, which means her news made the local newspapers and television. Mya didn't say it, but that's when she decided popularity was easier to attain than scholarships."

Liam removed his hat, then scratched his head. "But the thing I'm struggling with, is why Nia excelled and Mya didn't. They have the same genes, so they should be equally smart."

"I guess, but sometimes smarts don't play into it. In high school, as you know, you get different classes. This really started as a schedule problem; Nia got classes she loved, and studied hard. Mya wasn't so lucky, and didn't put in the effort," Charly was saying when someone started knocking on the door.

Liam put his hat back on, then stood. He put his finger to his mouth to quiet Charly, but he didn't have to. With the first knock, she hushed. "One second. I'm almost done in here," he yelled out.

The person kept banging on the door as if Liam hadn't spoken.

"Give me a second, please," Liam yelled louder.

Mumbling could be heard from outside, but Charly couldn't match the sounds to a particular person, not even their sex. "Give you a second or y'all?" Rory's voice bellowed. "Mya's out here, and we know Charly's in there." More mumbles sounded. "C'mon out, Charly."

Charly was stuck. She knew she had to face Rory, Mya, and Trent, but she couldn't. Not yet. It wasn't that she was afraid; she had to get to Nia. She had to talk to her, get to the root of some things, and hopefully dig up weeds that had infiltrated her happiness and her and Mya's relationship. She knew if she could do that, she would be able to plant new seeds that would give her the confidence to be outgoing and make Charly's mission complete. She looked at Liam, then to the walls, scouting for a window she could fit through and not be seen. "Over there. I need you to help me sneak out."

Liam was dumbfounded. "You don't need to be scared, love. I got you. I won't let anything happen to you. You know that, don't you?" He winked.

"I know," she assured him. "But I have to get to Nia. If I have it out with them, she may overhear more than she already has. That's what just happened, right? So help me please," she said, walking toward one of the windows. She stopped, then turned around. "And Liam?"

"Yes, love?" he asked, following behind her.

"Don't be looking at my booty either." She smiled.

23

Charly was out of breath. She'd slid out of the window, then run like she'd stolen something. She'd skirted the pool house, G.I. Janed her way through the bushes that stretched from the backyard to the side of the house, then gone through the front door and up the main staircase, only to have to turn around. She'd forgotten that the girls had their own set of stairs, and she wouldn't forget again, not after the way her aching feet kept reminding her with each throb. Finally, she'd hustled through the house and up to Nia's room. Before her hand knocked on the door, Nia opened it. Charly bent over, resting her hands on her knees. She felt like she'd just finished a marathon.

Nia stood quiet and motionless as if she were waiting for something major to happen while Charly tried to catch her breath. Then, as if nothing different was taking place, as if having a television reality star doubled over in her room was normal, she turned on her heels and walked over to her desk and sat down. She kicked up her heels on the desk, then turned and looked at Charly. "I guess Mya's won you over too," she said, her tone reminding Charly of how Heaven's had sounded. There wasn't an ounce of life to it. It just was.

Charly looked up, then gathered her strength. She took baby steps to Nia's bed and collapsed across the foot of it. She faced the ceiling, still panting. "I don't know so much about winning me over. *Convinced* would be a better word." Charly turned and looked at Nia. "Does that bother you?"

Nia shrugged. "Why would it? It's usual. Everyone likes Mya, eventually. Even the ones who start out hating her end up loving her. We're only twins by appearance . . ." She drifted off, then touched her face. "Well, we used to be, but that's it. We're day and night, oil and vinegar, heaven and hell. That's how the family describes us," she said, staring at the wall.

Charly rolled over onto her stomach, then propped herself up on her elbows, her chin in her palm. "And which would you be? Day or oil and heaven or night, vinegar and hell?" Charly asked. She was curious which category Nia would identify with. Did she view herself as positive and Mya as negative?

"Depends on who you ask, Charly. My dad would say Mya's day, oil and heaven, and our mother would say I was," she said, still staring into space.

"I'm asking you, Nia. Which one are you?"

Nia said nothing for almost a minute. So Charly tried again. "Okay, maybe it'll be easier to categorize your sister. Is she day, oil and heaven or night, vinegar and hell? Is she good or bad?"

Nia spun around in her chair to face Charly. "She used to be good, way back when. When she was still herself and not trying to be like other people, she was happier, nicer. She was my sister." Nia voice tapered off, and the look she wore was laced with hurt and regret.

"But she's still your sister, Nia." Charly slid off the bed, then walked over to where Nia was sitting, and sat on the floor. She looked up at her. "And she loves you. She does." Charly held up her hands, making quotation marks in the air. " 'I love Nia,' she said." Charly nodded. "She and I had a long talk, and you know what? Just like you think she gets all the attention and everyone loves her, she felt the same way when you were getting all the light for being so smart when she was struggling."

Nia lit. She sat up superstraight and scooted to the edge of the chair. Her brows rose, and she stopped blinking. "What do you mean by *struggling*? Mya never struggled in school, she just stopped going to classes."

Charly shook her head. "No, that's not what she said. You may not have known—I don't think anyone did." Charly wasn't one to divulge information that she'd been trusted with, but this time it was different. She had to accomplish her mission of remaking Nia from the inside out, but even more important than that, she realized, she had to help the sisters heal, and that would require her breaking her promise to Mya to keep her secret. "Nia, what I'm about to tell you, you have to promise me that you'll never tell. Do you hear me?" Nia nodded. "I mean it. Never. Say. A. Word. Promise!"

"I promise." Her gaze bore into Charly's eyes. "What is it?"

Charly gulped. She'd always prided herself on keeping her silence. For her it wasn't golden, like some said. It was more than that. Someone told you something and you forgot about it. It was that simple. Usually. "Mya is hiding behind her popularity. She doesn't feel as smart as she used to be. She said it was like one day none of it made sense. The AP calculus, AP chemistry, and something about switching to French from Spanish."

"Yes!" Nia interrupted. "I never understood that. She chose French, and I didn't get it. She'd always spoken Spanish, but then when we got to high school, she switched."

Charly nodded in agreement. "That's what she said. She said she switched languages, and couldn't switch back. The school wouldn't let her, and, after she saw how you were excelling, and everyone was so proud of you, she couldn't bring herself to admit she needed help. I guess you two never needed help before," Charly said, feeling a little jealous. She'd always struggled with at least one subject, so she didn't understand their long streak of near genius, but she'd witnessed it in her sister so she knew it existed.

Tears trekked down Nia's face at full speed. She shook her head. "So you mean to tell me that all this time my sister was hating me, it was because she was struggling with her classes?" Nia looked numb at the news that her twin could have something major like this happen, and she be totally in the dark. "I would've helped her, Charly. All she had to do was ask—hint—anything. But she didn't. She—"

"Ran to popularity. It was the easier choice," Charly assured.

Nia shook her head. "What did I do? What have I done? She's hated me, and made my life awful." Nia looked up at Charly. "I'm going to pay her back, Charly. I'm definitely going to pay her back."

Charly froze. She didn't know what to do. Here, she thought she was making progress, and she wasn't. Nia wanted retaliation. Retaliation for what? What happened to sympathy? "No, Nia. Not that."

Nia nodded. "Yes, just that." She got up from the chair. "Charly, I need a moment. Will you please leave?" Nia asked, then walked toward the bathroom.

Charly cleared her throat. "Well, are you still going to help me with your father's makeover?" she asked, not knowing what else to say.

Nia looked behind her. "I told you I would, right? You're confusing us twins again, Charly. I know your crew's setting up, and we have to make nice for the audience and the cameras. I know how to pretend to be a normal, happy family. I've been doing it for years. I told you I would help, and I am. I don't go back on my word."

Charly nodded, whipping out her phone. She texted Liam to come meet her. She knew she had to come face-to-face with Rory, Mya, and Trent, and after the way things had turned out with Nia—completely opposite of how they were supposed to—she didn't know what to expect.

24

When Charly and Nia walked out the back door and into the yard, they were all standing there, staring at her. Rory stood behind Trent, and Mya was next to him. Mya's arms were crossed, Rory's expression said she was livid, and disappointment masked Trent's face. Charly eyed them all, while the cast and crew finished setting up around them.

"Well?" Charly said, breaking the silence. The way Rory had demanded she come out of the pool house, she'd expected to be throwing blows by now, but nothing was happening. But just in case, she'd snatched her tendrils tightly and stepped out of her summer sandals. "Well?" she asked again, her neck snaking with attitude.

Trent stepped forward. "Charly, you've got a lot of nerve. I thought you were different. All you care about is camera time. You don't care about any of us."

Liam, who was standing next to Charly, walked around

her and came face-to-face with Trent. He appeared cool, but Charly knew better. Somewhere behind that beautiful face of his, his teeth were clenched. He reached up, then twisted his baseball cap backward, which Charly knew meant business. The only time she'd seen Liam do that before was when he really had to concentrate. "Trent, you good? We need to talk one on one, man to man?" he asked, his expression serious.

Trent nodded, but said, "No, Liam. I'm not good, and you wouldn't be either." He tsked, then spat on the ground. He looked over at Charly. "Do you think because we're from a small town that means we're slow, or do you just lie to and on everybody, Charly? Is that it?" he inquired, ignoring Liam asking him if they needed to talk man to man.

Mya's eyes began to water, and she wiped them. "Yes, Charly. Is that it?" Her voice cracked and rose with each word. "Because I'd like to know. Really know. Here I was thinking we were cool, thinking that I could trust you—telling you *every*thing and thinking you were my girl—and you'd lied on me to Trent. I'd never leave Trent stranded."

Rory opened her mouth to speak, and Charly held up her hand. She knew she was wrong, but she wasn't going to just stand in front of the firing squad without fighting back. "Well, that's not really true, Mya." She looked at Rory, slicing her hand through the air. "And Rory, don't even comment on it. Our wrongs cancel each other's out." She turned back to Mya, feeling that it was her she needed to appeal to the most. Mya had been right; they'd developed some sort of relationship while hanging out, and Charly didn't want her to think it was all a game. Charly did like her now that she'd gotten to know her better. "Can we talk inside the pool house? There are too many ears out here, and I don't think it's a good idea for the cast and the rest of the adults around here to know about your candy habits," she said, referring to the Skittles party, and hoping it'd make a difference, but it didn't.

"Who cares?" Rory boomed, making the backyard freeze and everyone within earshot turn their attention toward them. "So what if we have Skittles parties? Who doesn't?" she began.

Mya stepped on her foot. "Shuddup, Rory! You might not care, but I do. Just because your family is different . . ." She paused. "Never mind. Just don't forget who my dad is," she said, then began taking the few steps toward the pool house.

Rory snatched Mya back by her arm, twisting the sleeve of her shirt. She was in her face with spittle flying out of her mouth before anyone could stop her. "And what does that mean? Huh, Mya? What ya tryna say? 'Cause last time I checked, your family was just as messed up as mine. Just because your dad is the mayor don't mean y'all ain't got problems. Just look at the way you treat your sister, and after the way you wrecked her face."

Mya pushed Rory off her, then Charly jumped between them. To distract the ever-growing audience that was trying to see what was going on, she laughed loud and carefree, eyeing Liam to follow suit. She couldn't let anyone at the house know what was going on. She wouldn't dare expose the other teens or herself. If Mr.

Day had gotten a whiff of what she'd done, the lies and manipulation she'd worked to uncover secrets, she knew he'd snap from the smell of it, and would call it for what it was: bull manure.

"Good one, good one," Liam said, laughing, then elbowing Trent to join in. Trent shook his head, obviously preferring not to front for the onlookers.

Rory glared at Charly, then at Mya. "I can't stand either one of you think-you're-cuter-than-everybody heifers," she said, then pushed past Charly, grabbing for Mya.

Charly stood there with her eyes bulging. She didn't know what happened or how it occurred, but something had indeed transpired. Something quick and hard flashed in front of her eyes before she could make it out, and suddenly Rory was facedown on the ground. Charly's gaze went from Rory's back, to the foot pressed against it, then traveled up the person's leg it belonged to. "Nia?" she questioned.

"Nia?" Mya was shocked.

"Rory, we're cool, but don't you ever, and I do mean ever, push up on my sister," Nia fumed, then looked at Mya. "Are you all right?"

Mya, eyes bigger than the sky, nodded. "Yes, Nia. I'm fine."

"Well, I'm not!" Rory yelled from under Nia's foot. "Get off me or let me up. Something!"

Charly made her way to Nia, then laced her arm through hers. "C'mon, let's go inside the pool house and talk." She looked at Mya. "You too."

Nia locked eyes with Charly. "I told you I was going to pay her back. As you see, I didn't mean in a bad way."

Mya looked to the ground, then she shook her head. "That's okay."

"No, it's not okay," Rory yelled, getting up off the ground. "It's never been okay. I've been trying to get you two to get it through your thick skulls, but no," she sang. "You're definitely twins. Twin hardheads." She looked at Charly while rubbing her head. "Now do you see why I called the show? These two are a piece of work. They've been too busy trying not to be like the other when it's impossible. Smart? Yes, that they are. Cute?" She flip-flopped her hand. "Kinda, but not as hot as me. Hardhead? Yes. Yes. Yes. Triple yes. And it sickens me. I wish I had a sister my age that I could hang out with instead of a little bratty one," she admitted, looking back and forth between Nia and Mya. "Heck, I wish I had a family with an ounce of sense."

Charly just nodded. Rory was on a roll, and she knew Rory would keep talking as long as someone was listening. "Let's go, Nia and Mya," she said, opening the door to the pool house, then waiting patiently while the sisters walked inside.

"Trent, let's go talk," Liam said. "There's so much more going on here than girl stuff."

Charly closed the door behind them, then locked it to prevent Rory from entering. Charly leaned against the wood, crossed her arms, then ping-ponged her eyes between the sisters. "Okay, we're not leaving out of here until we get this settled. You"—she pointed at Mya— "blame her for all your troubles." She pointed at Nia. "And vice versa. Now let's get to the heart of this, twins, because you and I know that both of y'all are wrong."

Charly eyed them, then saw Nia fidget just a little. "Spit it out, Nia. Please hurry too because I have a show to finish, and you two are holding me up."

Nia shook her head. "I'm sorry, Mya—"

"Sorry for what?" Mya cut her off. "I'm the one who put you through it." She shook her head. "I didn't mean to . . . You know I'm sorry about the accident. I didn't mean for it to happen, and I definitely didn't want to see you shut yourself off from everyone."

"It's my fault, not yours," Nia said, stepping up. "It's all my fault, not yours," she repeated.

Charly nodded. She didn't know where this was going, but was glad to see some progress.

Mya froze, tilting her head. "What do you mean?"

Nia shrugged. "I was getting all the attention, and, it doesn't take a rocket scientist to figure out that you were just acting out to get attention too."

Mya just looked at her sister for a second, then shot a questioning glance to Charly. Charly shrugged. There was no way she was going to hang herself, and was glad Nia hadn't exposed that she'd shared Mya's revelation with her. Mya nodded, then walked over to her twin sister and embraced her.

Charly exhaled. "Finally! Now can we get to work, ladies?" she asked as loudly as she could to be heard over Rory's knocking on the door.

Mya let go of Nia and smiled. "Yes. I'll do what I can, but I remember my dad telling me to stay out of the way."

Charly nodded in agreement, remembering when she'd snapped on Mya for not wanting to help. "Okay. Go see what Rory wants then." After Mya walked out, Charly turned to Nia. "Explain. It wasn't supposed to be that easy, and there has to be a reason you just caved like that."

Nia reached into her pocket, then pulled out half a red wrapper with white lettering. Charly's brows rose. She remembered seeing a corner of it tucked in Nia's room the first day she'd been in her room, but had forgotten all about it. Now it all made sense. "The night at the party . . . The accident . . ." Nia shrugged. "Mya wanted to stay and I didn't. I figured if she wanted to party with her new friends she should really party with her new friends. It was a Skittles party, so I crushed one up in her drink. We crashed because I drugged her," Nia admitted, batting her eyes slowly, unsuccessfully attempting to keep her tears from falling. "I'll never admit it though, Charly. I can't."

Charly looked at Nia. "You put the other half under my hotel room door? Was that you, Nia?"

Nia nodded, walking across the room and sitting on a chair. She exhaled. "You'd never guess how easy it is to know what's going on when you never leave the house, Charly. Especially when you've got loud-mouth friends like Rory."

"She was just looking out for you, Nia. They all were," Charly defended.

"But *I* didn't want a makeover, Charly. I just wanted everyone to let me be. What's so wrong with being yourself just because yourself doesn't fit in with society's definition of normal? Plus, with having you around, I figured I'd be exposed, eventually. I mean, how could I hide with you snooping around and trying to make me over?"

Charly was floored. Here she was trying to help Nia, and Nia had been playing her all along. She shrugged. She couldn't say too much. Even Nia had given her a heads-up and tried to make her go away by sliding the Skittles wrapper under her hotel-room door. "Okay. Okay. Okay," Charly said. "I got it now. I get it!" She raised her voice. "But I've got a trick for you, Ms. Nia. You will get a makeover and you'll enjoy it. And you're going to be the best nerd there is on the planet for a minimum of two years or else."

"Or else what?" Nia asked, her brows high and wearing a look like she was daring Charly.

Charly held up her cell in the air, waving it back and forth. "Or else I'm going to play this voice recording for the world," she threatened, lying and smiling, hoping Nia believed her.

Epilogue

The camera lights were shining bright and the street was filled with spectators. All were there for the big reveal and clapping on cue when the light indicated they were on air. Charly stood with Liam by her side.

"*The Extreme Dream Team* has decided on doing something different this time—a thing our audience members at home are aware of, but something the great folks of Tallulahville, Minnesota, have no idea about. Right, Liam?" Charly said as perfectly as she could while smiling.

Liam nodded, then shrugged. "Well, Charly, you know that's not exactly true. The town's mayor was aware of what's going on, and what's going on has nothing to do with his office as the town has been led to believe."

Charly nodded, then jumped right in where she was supposed to, pausing only here and there as the spectators oohed and ahhed. She turned to her right, then waved her arm in the air as pictures of Nia flashed on the screen. Charly went into Nia's story, praised her for her grades and multiple scholarships, then talked about her un-selfish heart. "Ladies and gentlemen, let's bring her out," Charly said, clapping her hands.

Nia walked out from behind the crowd. She was made over and wore a huge smile. Charly waved for the cameraman and boom guy to follow her, then embraced Nia with the phoniest hug she'd ever given in her life. "Remember," she said into Nia's ear through clenched teeth. It was only one word, but it was a huge threat. She turned back to the camera. "Now, ladies and gentlemen, to give you an example of the reason Nia was nominated for this show," she began, then thrust the microphone into Nia's face.

Nia smiled, nodding and crying. "As everyone here knows, I'm an identical twin. My sister's name is Mya, and I want her to have everything I have because she de-serves so much more than what other people know—in-cluding her own car. So since I'm getting a full scholarship, I've decided to donate part of my savings to Mya's car, and half of my new wardrobe . . ."

Charly nudged Nia a little, then batted her eyes slowly. Nia was going to give her what she'd requested or Charly was going to deliver what she'd promised. No, she didn't have the main part of the conversation recorded, but she was able to get the end of it on a digital recording appli-cation on her phone. "Wow, that's great, Nia. So you're going to donate half of your savings to help pay for your sister's car?" Charly said into the camera, then turned and masked her sneer behind a genuine-looking smile at Nia, and held that same grin until the show had wrapped.

The cameras' lights died, the microphones were cut off, and Charly exhaled. She couldn't believe a nerd had played her like that, but it had happened. Still though, she smiled because, played or not, she'd succeeded with the makeover. She'd given Nia and Mya complete overhauls from the inside out, and through all the turmoil, commotion, and years of hurt, the sisters had even found a way to bond again.

Hands clapping pulled her attention. "Very good, love," Liam said, walking up to her with a huge smile on his face.

Charly gave a slight bow, then stood up, readying herself to speak, but she couldn't. She wasn't able to because Liam's lips pressed against hers very quickly, then drew back. "Wow! Why'd you do that?" she asked, looking around. The kiss wasn't a kiss kiss, but it was enough to make her heart race.

Liam winked. "I've never kissed a real star before."

Charly laughed. "Well, if I'd have known that was all it took, I'd have flexed my star power much sooner."

Liam wrapped his arm around hers. "Really? Let's go for a walk, and you can tell me all about it."

STAR POWER

Kelli London

ABOUT THIS GUIDE

The following questions are intended to
enhance your group's reading of
STAR POWER.

Discussion Questions

1. Charly was on a mission to make over someone from the inside out. Do you think that's possible or should you just accept someone for who they are?

2. Charly used methods that would be considered bullying tactics to get the information that she wanted. Because it was for the good of others, do you think it was appropriate or could she have come up with other ways? Discuss.

3. Has there ever been a time when you had to be manipulative to get what you wanted? If so, was it for your best interest or others'?

4. Mya and Nia's father seemed to play favorites. Do you think that his being there more for Mya helped to push Nia into depression? If he had been there for them equally, do you think Nia would've needed as much help?

5. Did Nia really need help or was she just being herself? How do you know if someone needs help or not?

6. Mya chose popularity over being her true self. Have you ever thought that popularity was more

appealing than being who you truly are? Why or why not?

7. While we know that doing drugs of any kind is wrong and dangerous, prescription medication and pill parties were discussed in the book because, unfortunately, their use has become a part of life for many. Drug use can lead to death, hospitalization, addiction and, as you've just read, accidents. Can you think of anything else drug use can lead to?

8. Should Charly have called the cops or an adult to report the Skittles party? Was she irresponsible for not doing so? Did she fall victim herself to popularity because she didn't, and snitching is frowned upon and, thus, not popular?

9. Because Mya had a habit of attending Skittles parties, was she addicted?

10. Who would you call if you learned of someone taking drugs? Do you know your local drug hotline? Would you be brave enough to report drug use?

Meet Charly for the first time in . . .

Charly's Epic Fiascos.

Available wherever books are sold!

This is going to be easy. Simple. "Turn. Turn. Turn!" Charly said, grabbing her little sister, Stormy, by the forearm. She shoved her hip into Stormy's side, forcing her thin frame to round the corner of the schoolyard. Her feet quickened with each step. They were almost home-free.

"Ouch!" Stormy hissed, cradling her torn backpack to her bosom like an infant in an attempt to prevent her books from falling onto the cracked sidewalk. "All this for Mason? Serious? Let go of my arm, Charly. Let me go. If I had known we'd be up here mixed up in drama, I wouldn't have come to meet you. I need to get home and study."

Charly rolled her eyes. Being at home is exactly where her sister needed to be. She hadn't asked Stormy to meet her. In fact, she remembered telling her not to come. She'd had beef with one of the cliques over nothing—not him, as Stormy thought. Nothing, meaning the girls were hating on Charly for being her fabulous self and for being Mason's girl. She held two spots they all seemed to want but couldn't have. She was the It Girl who'd snagged the hottest boy that had ever graced her town. "Go home, Stormy," she said, semi-pushing her sister ahead.

"Do it again and I'm going to—" Stormy began.

"You're going to go home. That's all you're going to do," Charly said matter-of-factly, then began looking around. She was searching for Lola, her best friend. If she had to act a fool, she'd prefer to show out with Lola around, not Stormy. She had to protect her younger sister, not Lola. Lola was a force to be reckoned with and she wasn't afraid of anyone or anything.

A crowd came her and Stormy's way, swarming around them as the students made their way down the block. A shoulder bumped into Charly, pushing her harder than it should have. Charly squared her feet, not allowing herself to fall. Quickly, she scanned the group, but was unable to tell who the culprit was. "If you're bad enough to bump into me while you're in a group, be bad enough to do it solo. Step up," Charly dared whoever.

Stormy pulled her as some members of the crowd turned toward them. "Come on, Charly. Not today," Stormy begged. "Remember the school said if you have one more incident you'd get suspended."

Charly grabbed Stormy's arm again, preparing to jump in front of her in case the person who pushed her stepped forward.

"Hey, baby," Mason called, pushing through the crowd. "Everything good?" he asked, making his way to her and

Stormy. "Or do we gotta be about it?" he asked, then threw a nasty look over his shoulder to the group. " 'Cause I know they don't want that." His statement was a threat, and everyone knew it. Just as Charly was protective over her sister, Mason was protective over her. His lips met her cheek before she could answer him.

"We're fine, Mason," Stormy offered.

Mason nodded. "Better be. They're just mad 'cause they're not you. But you know that. Right?"

Charly smiled. Yes, she knew.

"Good. Listen, I need to run back into the school for a minute," he said, reaching down for her book bag.

Charly hiked it up on her shoulder. "You can go ahead. We're good. I promise."

He stood and watched the crowd disperse and start to thin before he spoke. "All right. I'll catch up to you two in a few." He disappeared into the crowd of students still on school grounds.

"So really, Charly? You were going to fight whoever over him?" Stormy asked again.

Charly ignored the question as she focused on parting the crowd. They needed to get down the block.

"Hey, Charly! Call me later. There's something I want to talk to you about," a girl shouted from across the street.

Charly looked over and nodded. She couldn't have remembered the girl's name if she'd wanted to, let alone her number. Obviously the girl knew her though, but who didn't?

"Catch up with me tomorrow," she answered, then released her grip on Stormy and sucked her teeth at her sister's questioning. Stormy had no idea. Mason was the new guy around and the guy of her dreams. They'd been dating, but she couldn't let him know just how much he had her because then she'd be like every other girl in their town. And she refused to be like the others, acting crazy over a guy.

"Mason, Charly? That's what this is all about?" Stormy asked again.

"Shh," Charly said, shushing her sister. "What did I tell you about that? Stop saying his name, Stormy."

Stormy shook her head and her eyes rolled back in her head. "Serious? What, calling his name is like calling Bloody Mary or something? I *so* thought that Bloody Mary thing only worked with Bloody Mary's name and Brigette's generation. Who believes in such stuff, Charly? You can call anyone's name as many times as you like."

Charly got tense with the mention of their mother. Brigette refused to be called anything besides her given name, and Mom, Mommy, and Mother were definitely out of the question. That she'd made clear. On top of that, she insisted her name be pronounced the correct *French* way, Bri-jeet, not Bridge-jit.

"Please don't bring her up. My afternoon is already hectic enough. I don't wanna have to deal with Brigette until I have to," Charly said, her quick steps forcing rocks to spit from the backs of her shoes. "Just c'mon. And, like you, I need to get my homework done before I go to work. Mr. Miller said if my math assignment is late one more time, he'll fail me. And I can't have that. Not right before we go on break for a week. And I don't want to do any sort of schoolwork while we're out. Oh!" She froze.

A dog ran toward them at top speed from between two bushes, then was snatched back by the chain leash around its neck. It yelped, then wagged its tail, barking. Charly, a little nervous, managed strength and pushed Stormy out of harm's way. Looking into the dog's eyes, she was almost afraid to move. She'd distrusted dogs since she was five, when her mother had convinced her they were all vicious, and now her feelings for them bordered on love/hate. She'd loved them once, and now hated that they made her uncomfortable, but was now determined to get over her fear. A pet salon near her home was hiring, and, whether she liked dogs or not, she needed more money for her new phone and other things.

The wind blew back Charly's hair, exposing the forehead that she disliked so much. Unlike Stormy, she hadn't inherited her mother's, which meant on a breezy day like today, her forehead looked like a miniature sun, a globe as her mother had called it when she was upset. On her mom's really peeved days, which were often, she'd refer to Charly as Headquarters. Charly smoothed her hairdo in place, not knowing what else to do.

Stormy grabbed her arm. "C'mon, Charly. We go through this at least twice a week. You know Keebler's not going to bite you, just like you know he can't break that chain." She shrugged. "I don't know why you're so scared. You used to have a dog, remember? Marlow . . . I think that's the name on the picture. It's in Brigette's photo album."

Charly picked up speed. Her red bootlaces blew in the wind, clashing against the chocolate of her combats. Yes, she'd had a dog named Marlow for a day, then had come home and found Marlow was gone. Charly had never forgotten about her, but, still, she'd believed her mother then, and now couldn't shake the uneasiness when one approached. Especially Keebler. He'd tried to attack her when he was younger, and she still feared him. So what if he'd gotten old? Teeth were still teeth, and dogs' fangs were sharp. "How do you know he won't bite, Stormy? You say that about every dog."

Stormy laughed, jogging behind her. "Well, Charly. Keebler's older than dirt, he doesn't have teeth, and that chain is made for big dogs, I'm thinking over a hundred pounds. Keebler's twenty, soaking wet. What, you think he's going to gnaw you to death?"

Charly had to laugh. She'd forgotten Keebler was minus teeth. "Okay. Maybe you're right. We only have two more blocks," she said, slowing her walk. Her pulse began to settle when she caught sight of the green street sign in the distance, and knew she'd soon be closer to home than barking Keebler. "Only two more and you can get to your precious studying, nerd," she teased Stormy, who laughed. They both knew how proud Charly was of Stormy's intelligence. Stormy didn't hit the books because she needed to; she had to, it was her addiction. "And I can knock out this assignment," she added.

"Yo, Chi-town Charly! Hold up!" Mason called, his footsteps growing louder with each pound on the concrete.

Charly picked up her pace. She wanted to stop but she couldn't. Boyfriend or not, he had to chase her. That's what kept guys interested. Stormy halted in her tracks, kicked out her leg, and refused to let Charly pass. "What's going on now? Why are you ignoring Mason? Oops, I said his name again." Stormy sighed, pushing up her glasses on her nose.

Charly rolled her eyes. "I'm not really ignoring Mason, Stormy. Watch and learn—I'm just keeping him interested," she said, failing to tell her sister that she was trying to come up with an explanation for disappearing the weekend before. She'd told him she was going to visit her family in New York, and now she just needed to come up with the details. Her chest rose, then fell, letting out her breath in a heavy gasp. What she'd hoped to be a cleansing exhale sputtered out in frustration. "He may be a New Yorker, but we're from the South Side of Chicago. I got to keep the upper hand." She repeated the mantra she used whenever she had to face a problem, but it was no use. The truth was, yes, they had been born on the South Side of Chicago, but now they lived almost seventy miles away from their birthplace in an old people's town. She couldn't wait to leave.

Mason's hand was on her shoulder before Charly knew it. She froze. Turning around was not just an option; she had to. She knew that he knew that she'd heard him now. Summoning her inner actress, she became the character she played for him. Charly switched gears from teenage girl to potential and future Oscar nominee. She erased the glee of him chasing her down from her face and became who and what he knew her to be. Cool, calm, self-assured Charly—the girl who seemed to have it all. Seemed being the operative word since she lacked teen essentials like the Android phone she was saving for and a computer.

"Hey! I said hold up. Guess you didn't hear me. Right?" His voice was rugged and his words seemed final, as if he had nothing else to say. His tone spoke for him. It was sharp and clipped, yet something about it was smooth. Just hearing him speak made her feel good.

She smiled when she turned and faced him. "Hi, Mason. I'm sorry. There's so much wind blowing that I couldn't hear you."

Mason smiled back and did that thing with his eyebrows that made her melt every time. He didn't really raise or wiggle them, but they moved slightly and caused his eyes to light. "Yeah. So . . ." he began, then quieted, throwing Stormy a *please?* look.

"Okay. Okay. Personal space. I get it," Stormy said, then began to walk ahead of them. "You high schoolers are sickening."

Mason smiled at Stormy's back, and Charly grimaced behind it. She hadn't asked Stormy to give her and Mason alone time, and wished that her sister hadn't. The last thing she wanted was to be alone with Mason because every time she was, her lies piled. They'd stacked so high that now she couldn't see past them, and had no idea how to get around or through them.

"So, I've been trying to catch up with you to see how New York was last weekend when you went to visit your pops. You did fly out for the weekend, right?" he asked, his eyes piercing hers like he knew she hadn't gone.

She scrunched her brows together. It was time to flesh out her partial untruths. She thought of her semi-truths that way because to her they were. She'd done and been and imagined it all in her head, so, in a way, her not-so-trues were kind-of-trues.

"Uh, yeah." *Here comes the hook*, she thought while she felt the fattening lie forming on the back of her tongue, pushing its way out her mouth. "Right. But it was no biggie. I wasn't even there a whole two days. I was in and out of Newark before I knew it. I visited my dad and my aunt. She works for a television station—where they film reality shows. One day I'm going to be on one. That's the plan—to become a star."

"Newark? That's Jersey. I thought you said you were flying into Queens." He looked at her, pressing his lips together. He'd totally ignored her star statement.

"Queens? Did I say Queens?" *Dang it*. She shrugged, trying to think of a cover.

"Yep. You said your pops was picking you up at La-Guardia airport. That's in Queens. Guess Newark was cheaper, huh?" He waved his hand at her. "Same difference. Me and my fam do it too. Sometimes it pays to fly into Jersey instead. It's about the same distance when you consider traffic time instead of miles."

Charly nodded, pleased that Mason's travel knowledge had saved her. "Yeah. I know that's right. And I got there when traffic was mad hectic too. I'm talking back to back, bumper to bumper. But it was cool though. Manhattan's always cool, Brooklyn too," she lied about both. She'd never been to Manhattan and she was only five when she'd visited Brooklyn. But she'd gone to places like Central Park and Times Square all the time in her mind, and a mental trip to the Big Apple had to count for something.

"Brooklyn, yeah, it's cool. Matter of fact, I miss home so much, I just got a puppy and named her Brooklyn." He smiled.

Charly raised her brows. "Really? That's hot. I just love dogs. In fact, I just applied for a gig working at the pet salon." Another partial lie. She had planned on applying, she just hadn't had time yet.

Nodding in appreciation, his smile grew. "That's good, Charly. And it couldn't have come at a better time." He took her book bag from her, then slung it over his shoulder. "Dang. This is heavy. What'chu got in it?"

"Math," Charly said. "I got to ace this assignment, so I brought home my book and every book the library would let me check out to make sure I get it right. Because I go to New York so much, I kind of fell behind on the formulas," she added. She couldn't have him think her anything less than a genius.

Mason nodded. "Good thinking. Knock it out from all angles. Math is the universal language. Did you know that?" he asked, but didn't give her time to answer. "Let's walk," he said, clearly not letting up. "It must be nice to have your pops send for you a couple times a month. So what'd you do all weekend? Party?"

She kicked pebbles out of her way, wishing they were

her lies. She hadn't seen her father since she was five, and it was something that was hard for her to admit, especially since Stormy's dad was still on the scene for birthdays and holidays. The truth was she had no idea where her father was, so she imagined him still living in New York, where she'd last seen him.

"So did you party?" Mason repeated.

Me, party? Yeah, right! My mom partied while I worked a double shift to save for a new phone. Then I sat holed up in the house on some fake punishment. "Yeah, actually I did. Nothing big though. It was a get-together for my aunt. You know, the one I told you about who's a big shot at the network. Well, she just got promoted, and now she's an even bigger big shot. She's got New York on lock."

Mason nodded, then slowed his pace as Charly's house came into view. "That's cool, Charly. Real cool. It's nice to finally have a friend I can chop it up with. Ya know, another city person who can relate. Somebody who gets where I'm from. Not too many people around here can keep up with my Brooklyn pace," he said, referring to the almost-dead town they lived in. Their tiny city was okay for older people, but teens had it bad. They lived in a nine-mile-square radius with only about twenty-five thousand other people. There was only one public high school and one emergency room, which equated to too small and everybody knowing everyone else and their business. Nothing was sacred in Belvidere, Illinois.

Charly took her book bag from Mason. "Trust me, I know. They can't keep up with my Chi-Town pace either. I'm getting out of here ASAP."

He walked her to her door. "Speaking of ASAP. You still gonna be able to come through with helping me with my English paper this week? I have to hand it in right after break, so I'd really like to get it finished as soon as possible. Don't wanna be off from school for a week and have to work." He shrugged. "But I know you're pressed with school and getting an A on the math assignment. Plus, with flying back and forth to New York to check your pops, and trying to work at the pet salon, I know you're busy. But I really need you, Charly," he paused, throwing her a sexy grin that made her insides melt. "I don't even know what a thesis statement is, let alone where one goes in an essay."

Charly smiled, then purposefully bit her tongue to prevent herself from lying again. She'd forgotten when Mason's paper was due. An essay she would be no better at writing than he would. She sucked in English, but couldn't pass up the opportunity to be close to him. "I gotta work tonight and pretty much all week," she said. She was finally kinda sorta truthful. She did have to work. Now that she was sixteen, and had snatched up a job at a local greasy spoon—and, hopefully, the pet salon she'd told him she had applied at—it was up to her to make sure that the electric and cable bills were paid, plus she had to pay for her own clothing. "We've been *very* busy at work, for some reason."

"Okay." Mason grimaced, then looked past her, apparently deep in thought. He rubbed his chin. "I don't know what I'm going to do now. I gotta pass this class. . . ."

Charly pressed her lips together. She couldn't let him down. It was because of her that he'd waited so long to tackle the paper. She'd told him not to worry, that she had him, that she was something like an A or B English student. Now, it'd seem as if her word was no good, and she couldn't have that.

"Kill the worry, Mason. I'll work it out."